The Best-Kept Secret
Adrianne Lee

HARLEQUIN®

TORONTO • NEW YORK • LONDON
AMSTERDAM • PARIS • SYDNEY • HAMBURG
STOCKHOLM • ATHENS • TOKYO • MILAN • MADRID
PRAGUE • WARSAW • BUDAPEST • AUCKLAND

To Betty Ann Patterson, who believed in me when I needed it, and who gave me back my dream.

THANKS

Dave Tilbor, VP Marketing Services at Galoob Toys in San Francisco; Sharon Anderson, Director of Human Resources at Irwin Toy Limited in Toronto; and Judy Strege, great writer and friend; and always, Anne Martin, Kelly McKillip, Susan Skaggs and Gayle Webster.

ISBN 0-373-22496-6

THE BEST-KEPT SECRET

Copyright © 1998 by Adrianne Lee Undsderfer

"I won't let anything happen to you."

Mac gathered Tia to his bare chest, and the nightmare faded as she pressed her cheek near his heart. He gently rubbed her back through her T-shirt, his hand moving in slow, soothing strokes.

"It'll be okay, Tia."

She wanted to believe him, but he didn't have all the facts. Her nightmares weren't dreams. They were reality in the world of Tia Larken.

As the moments passed, her pulse hummed faster. Her anxiety diluted into something sweet—and forbidden. The thrum of Mac's heart sent blood rushing through her veins with sizzle and promise.

She lifted her head and found him gazing down at her. He lowered his mouth to hers. The kiss sent ribbons of passion floating through her, soft and silken. She reached her hands around his neck to pull him closer, letting him know she wanted this. Wanted more.

She knew they had to stop, or Mac would regret this. But pleasure dragged his name from her parted lips. "Oh, Mac. Mac…please stay.…"

Dear Reader,

Hi, all. As far back as I can remember my mother was an avid reader of mystery, and her tastes in books helped me shape my own. So I think it is only fitting that I now have her reading and enjoying Harlequin's wonderful Intrigue line. Thanks, Mom.

I wish you all a happy and loving holiday with just a sweet pinch of mystery to keep it interesting. I love hearing from readers. Reach me at: P.O. Box 3835, Sequim, WA 98382. Please enclose an SASE for response.

Adrianne Lee

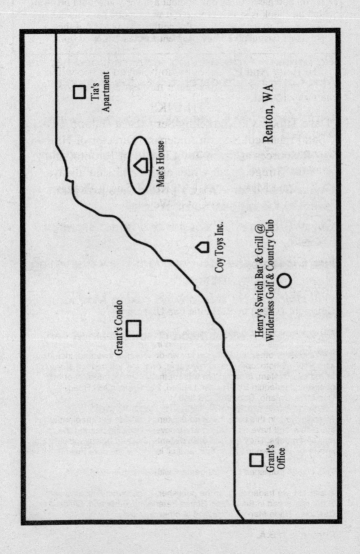

Tia's
Apartment

Mac's House

Renton, WA

Coy Toys Inc.

Grant's Condo

Henry's Switch Bar & Grill @
Wilderness Golf & Country Club

Grant's
Office

CAST OF CHARACTERS

Tia Larken—A devastating secret changed her life.

Mac Coy—His life depended on the woman he secretly loved.

Grant Coy—The P.I. masqueraded as his twin—and died for it.

Suzanne Chang—Nothing the head of marketing said rang true.

Gwen Gallagher—Mac's trusted vice president revealed the biggest surprise of all.

Ginny Gibson—Tia's best friend had a secret of her own.

Bud Gibson—The security guard knew everything about Tia's past...almost.

Will Holden—He was always asking Mac for more money.

Bijou Novak—Mac's head of sales seemed very nervous.

Nancy Rice—Mac's assistant liked his new look—a *lot*.

Stewart Stewicki—A helpful, concerned employee?

Fred Vogler—The operations manager had a thing for matches.

Chapter One

The man on the sofa stared at the television, his chest heaving with grief.

"Today in a bizarre accident," the newscaster said, "local toy manufacturer Mac Coy died when a virtual reality simulator he was testing shorted out, electrocuting him."

The anchorwoman wore a Christmas-green suit with a silver Santa on her lapel. The set around her sported pine boughs sprinkled with tiny white lights and tied with plaid ribbons. The decor conveyed the warmth of the holiday, while the anchorwoman's words, spoken in a flat and emotionless tone, sliced the man's heart like a jagged edge of a shattered tree ornament.

Maybe it was the tree across the room, the decorations all around him, that made him feel connected to her, but he could swear she stared directly at him, speaking to him alone, as though they were captured in some lost Yuletide episode of "The Twilight Zone." "No one is quite sure how this happened."

The man was dead certain how it had happened. Murder. Murder made to appear accidental. That VRS had been rigged. He tossed back a shot of Cuervo Gold.

The newscaster continued, "A spokesman for Coy Toys said that Mr. Coy's death is even sadder coming as it has at this time of year with the company's impending release of a revolutionary breakthrough in the industry."

The man laughed, a bitter, pained, mirthless burst of noise that echoed off the living-room walls. Holly Beary's Heart, a breakthrough meant for the good of the world. For the joy of children everywhere. Instead, it had fostered industrial espionage. And now murder. His insides ached with cold, as though he'd swallowed a block of ice.

The newscaster shuffled the pages on her desk. "Mac Coy's brother, CEO of Quell Inc., Grant Coy, could not be reached for comment."

The man glanced at the phone, unplugged from the wall, and winced. His brother was dead. His twin. The other half of him. The better half. What the hell did the press expect him to say? That he was bereft? And angry enough, for the first time in his life, to commit a violent crime? To rip the murderer limb from limb?

If he had the faintest idea how to go about finding the murderer.

He clicked off the television set. The screen crackled in protest, then faded to black. The sudden silence emphasized his grief. His guilt. Gripping his glass tightly, he tossed the remote control aside and lurched to his feet. His head swam. The room spun. The miniature lights on the six-foot tree, the only illumination in the room, blurred.

He shook his head. Tequila splashed from his glass

down the front of him. He cursed, shrugged out of the T-shirt and wiped himself off with it.

He dropped back to the sofa and tossed down the rest of the drink. His third. No, fifth. No. Hell, he'd lost count. He didn't usually drink anything stronger than coffee. Didn't like dulling his wits. Now he no longer cared. He needed desperately to blunt his heartache. To blot out all thought.

Except revenge.

His gaze slid to the presents beneath the tree. To one gift in particular. The one to his brother from him—a silly joke gift, something his brother would never open. A laugh they would never share.

The knot in his throat grew. He brushed a hand over his newly short hair, for the first time in a week hardly noticing the different length, and poured another drink. He slumped on the sofa, his eyes riveted to the gift. He sipped the liquor, wondering how he was going to find out who'd killed his twin.

Afraid there was only one way he could.

"YOU'RE JUST AFRAID."

"Afraid?" Tia Larken scowled at her best friend and brushed her dark hair from her cheek with a nervous hand. The airport lounge reeked of Christmas cheer this Friday evening, the crowd as merry as the paper Santa coasters beneath their drinks. Competing with the revelers and a garland-crowned television—tuned to the eleven-o'clock newscast—which sat two feet from them, Tia raised her voice, repeating, "Afraid?"

Ginny Gibson nodded, setting a spike of her short red hair waving at the crown of her head. "Prewedding jitters."

Tia swallowed against the knot in her throat. She and Ginny had just landed from a week-long layover in Taiwan. Friends since their teens, they'd gone to flight-attendant school together and hired on with Air Orient five years ago. She'd expected Ginny to say she was "afraid" Grant would find out about her past.

But even Ginny didn't know the worst of her past.

A sigh slipped from Tia. If either of them knew the truth about her, they'd walk away and never look back. She'd die if she lost Ginny, but would she really mourn the loss of Grant? A month ago she'd have said a resounding yes. But lately she'd felt him slipping away—as though he *did* know her secret. Almost as though he had found someone else.

Or had her secret merely made her see Grant in a clearer light? A less-flattering light?

Her indecision on the matter had nearly driven her crazy the past week. If only she could open up to Ginny... Fear danced with the wine in her belly. No, she couldn't risk it. Besides, Ginny seemed preoccupied with her own secret worries. "It's not prewedding jitters."

"Sure it is." Ginny slurped the last of her hot buttered rum and asked the bartender for a second. She turned her ardent brown eyes back toward Tia. "Just like my cousin Brenda. The moment she said yes to her boyfriend, she became as nervous as a cat with new kittens and stayed that way a whole year until after the 'I do's' were said. Then whammo—" Ginny clicked her fingers "—she relaxed."

"Your cousin Brenda was always a ditz. I'm not nervous," Tia insisted, even though both could see the tremble in her hand. She glanced at the ring Grant had given her and frowned. The three-carat, pear-shaped diamond glinted like an icicle in the light thrown by the television. She pulled in a bracing breath. "Engagement rings are supposed to symbolize love, but…I'm not sure I love Grant."

"What?" Ginny gaped at her. "Grant Coy is every woman's fantasy come true. He's easy on the eyes, keeps himself in great shape, is well-read, loves the arts, knows how to dress, earns a terrific living, is— according to you—fabulous in bed."

"Considering you've never met the man, you sure have a strong opinion of him."

"I've seen his photo, and I listen when you talk about him. And best of all, he's not a pilot. What more could you want?"

What more, indeed? Tia mused, knowing full well exactly what she wanted: to be someone else. "I can't marry a man I don't love."

Ginny sighed and gazed at her pointedly. "Aren't you just getting cold feet because you're a masochist who doesn't believe she deserves anyone so perfect?"

Not even someone half as perfect. Tia struggled to swallow her wine. She'd tried convincing herself it would work out, but from the moment she'd learned the truth about herself everything had changed. The ground had literally turned to mush beneath her feet. And every passing day reinforced the fact that Grant Coy deserved someone better than Tia Larken. Someone who was free to love him. Someone who loved him.

She glanced at the ring again, knowing it was only a matter of hours before she returned it. "I'm not looking forward to this evening."

"This isn't about that old business with Crimble,

is it?'' Ginny's brown eyes burned into her. '''Cause if it is, you should just tell Grant. If he's half the guy I think he is, he'll understand.''

She *had* told him about Crimble Industries. He *had* understood. But it was what she couldn't tell him that had her palms sweating. Her pulse beating erratically. If she really loved Grant, she would tell him the secret. Would *want* to tell him. Would *have* to tell him. But either way, the engagement was over. She'd found out she couldn't marry anyone. ''I wish it were that simple, Ginny. But some things in a person's past are insurmountable.''

''Phooey. If none of us can overcome our past, then I'm in huge trouble.''

Uneasiness sifted through Tia. If she didn't shift the subject a bit, Ginny would push and push to find out what in her past was so serious that she'd break up with Mr. Perfect over it. Better to let her think they were incompatible on an important issue. ''When we were in junior high, Ginny, do you remember how I described my ideal man?''

''Sure. He had to be sweet and make you laugh and he had to love kids.''

Kids. Yes. Tia's heart squeezed with such pain she could barely breath. *She* could never be a mother. But if she could, she'd want the father of her children to be someone more like Grant's brother than Grant. She gave Ginny a weak smile. ''When Grant and I met at the shelter last year, I was under the impression he *did* love kids. But lately I've begun wondering if it wasn't his brother who'd convinced him to volunteer. There's no doubt Mac Coy loves children. He's dedicated his lifework to them. He'd be a great dad.''

Tia thought of her own father and shuddered.

Ginny smirked and tapped the coaster with her index finger. "Sounds to me like your ideal man would be ol' Santa here."

Despite the solemnity of her feelings, Tia grinned. "Yeah, I guess that would be about right."

Ginny grew serious. "Are you actually going to break up with Grant three weeks before Christmas?"

Tia sighed. "I don't—"

"Oh, my God, Tia." Ginny interrupted, pointing to the tinsel-topped television. "Isn't that Grant's brother?"

Tia snapped her head around. Mac Coy's photograph filled the screen. She leaned closer, straining to hear.

The newscaster looked as though she sat in a Christmas card, an evil elf telling the boys and girls their favorite holiday had been canceled, that Mac Coy, their champion, had died. Tia gasped. Her heart constricted, then leaped inside her chest. "Mac... no...he can't be dead. This is awful."

Ginny covered her hand with her mouth, shock thick in her dark eyes, her face so pale her freckles stood out beneath her makeup. "Poor Grant."

Tia's misgivings collided with a burgeoning heartbreak. She lurched off the stool, laid a twenty on the bar and grabbed her purse and flight bag. She hurried out into the concourse. Her legs felt shaky and tears burned her eyes. Holiday travelers slewed past her like river water around a fish bent on swimming upstream.

"Where are you going?" Ginny asked a bit breathlessly as she fell into step beside her.

Tia shivered. "To Grant's."

"Have you decided what you're going to do?"

"Well, I'm certainly not going to break our engagement on the same day his brother died. I don't hate the man, Ginny. And right now, he needs me."

They stepped out into the rainy night. Buses and cars and taxis alternately parked and pulled away from the walkway. Tia told a porter she needed a cab, then stepped back to wait.

"Here comes my ride," Ginny said. She hugged Tia goodbye. "I'd be happy to find a man with half the promise of Grant Coy."

"You will." Tia assured her.

"I'm not holding my breath. God knows, my male role models haven't given me much to hope for in that area."

A car pulled to the curb. The driver was one of Ginny's three brothers. Tia couldn't tell which one through the darkly tinted, rain-streaked windshield. But it didn't matter; all three were as shady as a stand of giant elm trees.

ON THE RIDE from SeaTac International Airport to Grant's condo in Kennydale, Tia didn't hear the carols blaring from the cab's radio. How could she break up with Grant now? Grief surged again, washing away her concerns about the engagement like the rain spilling off the windshield of the car.

All that mattered right now was Mac had died. It seemed unreal. A bad dream.

A whole year had passed since they'd first met. Reluctantly, she dredged up old memories. At the homeless shelter last Christmas and into the ensuing two months, he'd been so good with the kids, always bringing new toys for them. Tia had thought him a bit of a nerd with his long hair and glasses, his baggy clothes, his awkward manner with adults.

But looking back now, she realized he'd been determined to bring some joy into the lives of those unfortunate children whose parents had fallen on bad times. Now she saw only his kindness. Why hadn't she noticed earlier? While he was still alive? While she could praise him for his dedication?

Anguish closed her throat. If she felt this upset, Grant would be inconsolable. Somehow, she would have to help him through this.

The taxi parked beside Grant's red Porsche. She paid the driver and hurried up the front walk of the two-story building. The wreath she'd given Grant hogged the top half of his door, looking too cheerful, too bright on this night of tragedy. A yuletide song began issuing from the decoration at her approach.

She cringed, her gaze dropping. A gaily wrapped present sat on the mat. She bent and picked it up. It fit her palm perfectly. The tag read, ''To Grant, from Santa.''

Frowning, Tia used her key to let herself into the condo. The unmistakable scent of pine engulfed her. The only light in the room came from the Christmas tree, soft, but sufficient. She glanced around the living room, orienting herself to sounds and sights, letting her eyes adjust.

The curtains stood open at the glass door, as though Grant had been standing there earlier looking out at Lake Washington. Rain pattered the roof and streaked the window. The knot in her stomach tightened. She locked the door, slipped off her shoes and coat, and left them beside her flight bag. Where was Grant now?

As if on cue, a gentle snore arose from the sofa. She found him slumped over, half-sitting, half-lying on the armrest. Her toe stubbed the heavy leaded cocktail glass overturned on the floor. Wincing in pain, she placed it on the coffee table next to the uncapped liquor bottle, set the present from Santa beside it, then sat next to Grant.

Her heart ached. She tapped his bare shoulder, speaking his name quietly. He rolled toward her, moaning. She pulled him into an awkward embrace, caressing his naked back, murmuring sympathetic nothings. He felt so warm, so vital, so alive. How could anyone he loved have died? Touching Grant now, she knew she had never wanted to make love to him so badly. To reaffirm his belief in life.

Or maybe she was the one who needed reassuring.

His head lolled back against her shoulder and his liquored breath fanned her face. Cuervo? She wrinkled her nose. Grant never drank tequila. His drink was gin. Besides a few bottles of expensive wine, it was the only liquor he kept in the condo. Where had he gotten it? A Christmas gift?

He moaned, slowly waking to her touch.

Feathering her hands across his smooth skin, she brought her palms to his chest and coiled her fingertips into the silken mat of hair. Something about this natural action struck a jangling chord deep within her grieving brain. She froze. Her eyes widened with the realization that what she was touching was not familiar. She yelped. Released him. This wasn't Grant. "Who are you?"

Scurrying to the opposite side of the sofa, her heart in her throat, Tia snapped on the end-table lamp. Terrified, she gaped at the man opposite her. Grant.

He squinted, peering at her through slitted eyes. Grant. Same short blond hair. Same turquoise eyes. Same dimpled chin. Despite that, she realized his chest was dappled with soft blond hair. Grant waxed his chest. Even if he'd decided to stop that practice, hair could not have grown this densely in the one week she'd been gone. This was *not* Grant.

Then who?

An awful truth slammed through her, numbing her. It could only be... But *he* was dead. Wasn't he?

"Mac?"

Chapter Two

Mac pried one eye open, squinting against the glaring illumination. The Christmas-tree lights blurred in the background, but he could swear the angel from its top now sat opposite him. A raven-haired, green-eyed angel. She seemed somehow familiar. But he couldn't connect the dots.

"Mac?"

Her voice rippled with horror. Why?

Recall sliced like a knife through his skull. His brother was dead. Murdered. The shock felt brand-new again, but the ache in his heart gave way to a stronger emotion: self-preservation. No one must know Grant had died in his place. If the killer discovered he or she had murdered the wrong man... But how could he convince this woman he was Grant? This woman of all women? "Tia, I—"

"If you're alive, Mac, then wh—?" She jammed her knuckles against her mouth, but not before emitting a squeal of pain. Denial and grief swam through the tears in her eyes. "No, not Grant..."

No, not Grant. It was what he'd been saying for hours like some baleful mantra. He touched his fingertips to his temples. His head ached from the liquor he'd ingested, but he felt as sober as if he'd drunk half a fifth of milk.

Beside him, Tia cried. Heavy tears spilled down her cheeks.

With every ounce of his being, Mac wanted to pull her into his arms, to hold to his heart the only other living person who understood his anguish. He reached a hand toward her, then pulled back self-consciously. His touch would only substantiate her identification of him. If he tried commiserating with her, he'd probably do or say the wrong thing. Women baffled him. Especially crying women.

Grant would have known how to comfort her. Would have convinced her he was Mac. And even though he believed with all his soul that pretending to be Grant was the only way to protect himself, Mac hadn't fooled Tia. Apprehension washed his gut. He likely couldn't fool anyone.

He wasn't Grant. Wasn't even like him in the ways that mattered. If he had been, this woman would have belonged to *him* and not to his brother. But that was the story of their lives. Grant always won top prize. He'd been talented, smooth, articulate, experienced.

While, Mac…well, he was just a bushy-bearded, long-haired, four-eyed, toy-making nerd. How would he ever avenge Grant's death—or save his company—if he couldn't fool people into thinking he was his twin?

Grant had been the sleuth, the master of disguise. He'd portrayed Mac so well… The thought choked him. *He'd played me so well, it had gotten him killed.*

"Why?" Tia's question scattered his dark thoughts. Her eyes were as green and wet against her pale face as grass through melting snow. "Why do you look so much like him?"

Mac blinked. Tia knew he and Grant were identical twins. That wasn't what she was asking.

He lifted his hand to stroke his beard. His fingers grabbed empty air, bumped his bristled jaw. He dropped his hand to his lap, disconcerted, embarrassed at his inability to cover his dismay. Another omen that he was doomed to failure if he thought he could trick people into believing he was Grant. "He…we…switched places. Last week."

"Yes." She nodded, obviously already deducing this. "But…why?"

Her tone implied that twins switching identities was childhood stuff, a teenage prank—not something grown men pulled.

Mac leaned forward, dropping his head into his hands. God, where did he begin? It seemed a lifetime ago. Had only seven days passed since his life had begun this downhill slide into hell?

"I hired Grant to find the spy in my company."

She swallowed as though she had an orange stuck in her throat, and he'd have sworn he saw alarm flit through her eyes. "The s-spy?"

Yes, spy. Even now he couldn't believe it—not of one of his handpicked employees. No! That wasn't true. He hadn't *wanted* to believe it. Not even when Grant insisted it must be true, not even when Grant insisted switching places was the only way to ferret out the mole. He shook himself, mentally shaking off the last vestiges of denial. A Judas walked amongst his most trusted. A murderer.

He sat back on the sofa. The leather felt cool against his bare skin, and he realized he was half-naked with his brother's fiancée, a woman he'd fallen in love with long before he'd introduced her to Grant. She'd been so great with the kids at the shelter. She'd owned his heart within the first week of their meeting.

He'd been too shy to act on his feelings. Besides, she hadn't ever given him a bit of encouragement. Then Grant had swept her off her feet.

Mac winced. He'd vowed to forget his feelings for her. To stop loving her.

If only his heart would listen.

The foolishness of falling for someone who would never return his affection embarrassed him, but the inappropriateness of those feelings—in light of Grant's death—shamed him. It was disloyalty at its worst. How could he even *think* about Tia—especially now—as anything more than a friend who shared his grief?

He found his shirt stuffed between the cushions that separated them. Heat warmed his ears as he grabbed it and tugged it on. "The toy we're about to launch," he said, shoving his hands through the armholes, grunting out the words, "I think someone sold its plans to an Asian competitor.

"A big manufacturer in Taiwan." He finished this last as his gaze cleared the neckline of the T-shirt.

Tia was swiping at her damp cheeks. Her glorious eyes gleamed like emerald ice melted at the edges. "What makes you think someone sold the plans?"

He forced his gaze from her face. It landed on the Christmas tree, on the gaily wrapped presents beneath. Some, he supposed sadly, were for Tia. He noticed a small box on the coffee table, the tag clearly marked, "To Grant from Santa." His heart clutched as much from grief as from the reminder of the present he'd received ten days ago. "I got a gift from Santa."

"What?" She tensed as though he'd made a tasteless joke.

But he was serious. "The box sported the logo of a Taiwan toy manufacturer, a company with a reputation for manufacturing ripoffs. It contained a sprig of holly berries."

Her smooth forehead puckered in a frown.

He rushed ahead. "'Holly Beary' is the name of the Christmas teddy bear we've designed and are launching next week."

Her eyebrows rose and something odd flew through her gaze. Alarm? Guilt? He couldn't tell. Had he imagined he'd seen one of those? Or both?

She said, "S-someone stole your patent?"

"I didn't want to believe it, but Grant—" He broke off. "I was wrong."

His throat felt dry. He glanced at the tequila bottle. God, he didn't want any more of that. All it had given him was an incredible thirst and a dull headache.

As though she'd read his mind, Tia lurched off the sofa. "Why don't I make us some coffee?"

As she stood, Mac couldn't help noticing how her airline uniform hugged her lush curves, how her thick black hair swished seductively across her shoulders and framed her alluring face. He reined in the onslaught of yearning that heated his blood. He would not shame them both with his inappropriate feelings. "Coffee sounds great. Thank you."

SOMEHOW THE TASKS of grinding beans and filling the drip coffeemaker with water, filter and some of Seattle's Best brought Tia the first sense of normalcy she'd felt since seeing Mac's photo on the airport television.

She was amazed she could stand, surprised her knees weren't wobbly. Shock, she supposed. The aroma of brewing coffee mingled with the soft scent of pine. Her heart felt shriveled and dark, a lump of coal left by a punishing Santa in some naughty child's stocking.

For the past seven days she'd done nothing but worry about whether or not she should marry Grant. Now he was dead. None of her concerns mattered any longer. Not her secret. Nothing. Except the fact that Grant had died because one of his brother's employees was a thief.

There were many kinds of thieves. Bitterness swelled inside her and grabbed her stomach with biting claws.

Trying to shake it off, she opened the cupboard and stared at the mugs she and Grant had bought last summer in Pike's Place Market. Each had a different photo of the Space Needle, the sight of their first date, emblazoned on its side. She set the mugs on the counter, recalling Grant's suggestion that they start buying pairs of mugs to commemorate their favorite outings.

Guilt dug the claws more deeply into her stomach. The overhead light glinted off her ring. She lifted her hand and stared at the diamond that was supposed to have symbolized their love. Her throat constricted. A mere hour ago she'd been prepared to return it to Grant. She'd felt it was the right thing to do. The only thing.

She wasn't worthy of him.

And even his death didn't change that.

Why hadn't she told him about herself as soon as she'd found out? Why had she held her silence for four long weeks? Why had she let him think she could spend a lifetime with him buying matching mugs? It was a lie.

The ring felt heavy on her finger, the diamond large and flawless, like a huge wedge of ice that might have been chipped from her frozen heart or her arctic conscience, her frigid guilt. If her love for Grant had been pure and honest, would he still be alive?

"That coffee done yet?" His voice sliced through her. The tone was Grant's, but somehow different.

She jerked toward him, stopping as suddenly as her gaze collided with his face—so familiar, the turquoise eyes, the strong straight nose, the even white teeth, the dimpled chin. It was like looking at Grant in a mirror, as though everything was somehow opposite or backward. It was Grant's face, but it wasn't. Something bitter, yet sweet, squeezed her chest, rattled her nerves.

She grasped the coffeepot handle with a trembling hand. Concentrating, she filled the mugs. She didn't want to lose control. Not again. She could confront her private demons when she was alone. Now she needed to make sense of this. And Mac had the answers. "Are you sure the Taiwan toy company actually *has* the plans for Holly Beary?"

"As sure as I can be without raiding their factory." He accepted a mug and took a drink. "Trouble is, to sue them means waiting until the release of their bear. Until then, I can't sic my lawyers on them. Or file suit. Not that I want to do either. Proving I'm right could take years—and wipe out whatever profit the toy might have brought."

He shook his head. "Coy Toys hasn't had a profitable toy in two years. I've been operating a heartbeat away from the red the last three months. I really need *this* toy to hit."

Pain flashed across his eyes, and she guessed he was thinking of Grant paying the ultimate price for a toy—a teddy bear of all things, the symbol of comfort and love. Before he could launch a litany of explanation, she raised a palm to him. "It was an accident. You can't blame yourself."

"Can't I?"

"No. Your concerns for your company are legitimate." She understood his concern more than he would ever know. "Grant is—was—a private investigator. You needed someone to investigate."

"Need."

"What?"

"You said 'needed.' Past tense. But Grant's death hasn't ended my need to unearth the spy. If anything, it was meant to slow me down. To let my competitor beat us to market with Holly Beary." He snapped his fingers. "Good God, I've got to move up the launch date. We've been working seven days a week. I think we can have the bears ready to ship by Friday. That gives us five days."

Tia cradled her mug in both hands. She leaned a hip against the counter and studied Mac's face long and hard. If he was under such a time crunch to launch this Christmas toy, what was he doing here hiding out in Grant's apartment? Wearing Grant's clothes, drowning his sorrow in tequila—instead of correcting the world's mistaken belief that *he* was dead? "Why does everyone still think *you,* and not Grant, died at Coy Toys today?"

He flinched as though she'd struck him, his eyes glistening with anger and grief. "Because whoever killed Grant—"

"K-killed?" Hot coffee sloshed onto her finger. She grimaced in pain and set the mug aside. She gaped at Mac.

No. Her insides felt gelid. "You think Grant was m-murdered?"

"That virtual reality simulator might have given someone a shock, but it wouldn't have killed anyone with a heart as physically sound as Grant's." His voice choked with rage. "Yeah, I think he was murdered. In fact, I'd stake Saint Nick's eight reindeer on it."

She blinked at the flippancy of his last words. It was something Grant would have said, not Mac. She supposed he'd used it to add weight to his accusation. To convince her. But his expression convinced her. Fear burned hot in her ice-clogged veins, sending a stinging sensation through her. "Are the police investigating?"

"They decided it was an accident. A frayed cord. I have no intention of trying to change their minds just yet."

A morass of unpleasant memories swelled in her brain. She knew the difficulty of changing a policeman's mind once it was set on a course. But this time was nothing like that time. No one had died then. No one could blame her for Grant. "Why not now?"

"Because they'll find out soon enough." Frustration spiked his words. "Too soon to suit. Then I won't be able to get rid of them."

Her mouth dried. She, too, knew how hard it was to get rid of the police once they got involved in a case. But even she knew they needed to be involved in this right now. "So they don't even know about the spy?"

"No."

"Why not?" She was incredulous. "Won't they realize something suspicious is going on when they discover Grant is wearing a wig and a false beard?"

Mac shook his head. "He didn't choose to fake my look. Instead, he donned some glasses and told everyone he'd decided to cut his hair and shave. I had to do that, in case someone came here expecting to find Grant."

"And none of your employees thought that was suspicious?"

"Not that I know of." Mac lifted his hand to the bridge of his nose, an unconscious gesture of someone used to nudging glasses back into place. But he wasn't wearing glasses.

He caught himself, looked momentarily disconcerted, as he had earlier when he'd reached to touch his beard. His missing beard. The tops of his ears reddened, and a thread of sympathy for this self-conscious man wound through her heart. She couldn't recall ever seeing Grant ill at ease. How could two men who looked so alike be so different? "So you didn't go to the police when you suspected you had a spy?"

"No. Grant said it would be better if we—he—sniffed the culprit out. Once we had proof, we'd take it to the police and let them handle it. But now…" He cleared his throat, carried his cup to the sink, dumped the contents and deposited the cup among the other unwashed dishes. His shoulders were slumped as though they carried the weight of the world. When he turned to face her, she read torment in his eyes. "I've been wrestling the problem all afternoon—trying to figure out how Grant would want me to handle it."

Suddenly she understood his dilemma. "When the police discover they have a murder case, they'll all but shut down the factory to investigate, and your wonderful toy won't meet its launch date. Is that it?"

"I know it sounds crass to put a toy—especially one that could make me extremely wealthy—above finding out who killed my brother, but actually it's not. Grant wanted Holly Beary launched. If I don't do this—"

"The killer wins on all counts," she finished for him. "You're right. Grant would never have forgiven you for that. And I suppose negative publicity could destroy the toy's chance of being a success."

"Yes." His relief at her understanding was palpable. "Besides that, the minute I confess I'm really alive, I'll be the prime suspect. The police always suspect relatives first."

Not always, Tia thought with a shiver. She set her mug in the sink beside his.

"I didn't kill Grant," he said.

"Oh, God, I never thought you did."

The sadness in his eyes reached inside her, locking onto a chunk of her heart with such a possessive grasp it sent a shock of heat to her toes. The kitchen seemed to shrink, grow smaller, more intimate, as though they were the only two people left in the world after a nuclear holocaust. She had never given Mac much thought. He'd always worn his blond hair long, pulled back at the nape with a leather thong, kept his eyes

obscured behind utilitarian glasses, hid his classic jaw
and its intriguing dimple beneath a scruffy beard.

So why was she noticing him now? Because of his
resemblance to Grant? Because of the connection they
shared in losing someone both had loved? Or was it
something more personal, more primal? Something
amiss in her basic personality structure that explained
this undeniable, and wholly wrong, need to be held
by her dead fiancé's brother?

Her lungs ached as though she hadn't taken a
breath in hours. The sensation unnerved her. She
stepped away from Mac, confused by her overwhelming urge to step into his arms instead.

He broke the heavy silence. "I want a look at that
simulator cord. It wasn't frayed last week."

"Oh, good idea." Tia nodded, glad for the first
suggestion of a course of action. She'd been up for
hours and ought to be asleep on her feet. Instead, she
felt stimulated. Too much coffee? Too much grief?
Too much intimacy with this kinder, gentler version
of Grant? "Could we go to your factory now?"

"We?" His blond eyebrows shot toward the ceiling. "No way."

"Why not?" Tia's temper seized on his chauvin-
istic tone. Maybe he was more like Grant than she
assumed. "Because I'm female?"

He frowned, not making the association. "No."

"Then why?" She felt as befuddled as he looked.
"I don't know about you, but right now I could use
a mental distraction."

"I understand, but I won't deliberately put you in
danger."

"Danger?" She crooked a lock of hair around one

ear. "Do you really think the killer will strike again if he or she believes you're dead?"

"If I'm caught inspecting the simulator—then, yeah, it's highly likely." His mouth firmed. "I want you to stay as far away from Coy Toys as possible."

Tia schooled her temper. Resignation and a finite sense of uselessness sifted through her. It was his business, his property. She couldn't argue with him. Why didn't she just go home?

She nodded. "Fine. I'll clean up these dishes for you, then call a cab."

She gathered the mugs, intending to put them in the dishwasher. But Mac caught her arm. His touch startled her, warmed her. Their gazes collided and the unspoken connection skipped a notch higher. He said, "Don't go."

His expression was bleak. Tia suspected he wanted help with funeral arrangements. A shiver slid down her spine. She supposed for his sham to work they'd have to stage a funeral for Mac. Naturally they'd hold the real one after the toy was safely on the market. "I know you have to continue letting the world think Mac Coy is dead—"

"Exactly," he said, releasing her, pulling back his warmth as surely as if he'd been embracing her. "I knew you'd understand. I have to *be* Grant for the next week or so. It's the only way to figure out who killed him without inciting another attempt on my life. And hopefully by the time the toy is safely in stores, I'll have found enough evidence to interest the police."

"So you want me to make the arrangements?"

He frowned, reached for his chin. Dropped his hand. "Arrangements?"

"For the funeral."

His face paled. "Oh, God. I hadn't thought of that. What... How...?"

He looked ready to crash again, as though anything veering from his mind-set was too much of a segue for him at the moment. She touched his hand. The contact sent a warm frisson up her arm, and she wanted to pull back. Couldn't. She swallowed hard. "I'll help you with the faux funeral, Mac, and the real one. We'll get through this together."

He tugged his hand free as though she'd burned him. "Thank you. But there won't be a funeral until the toy goes out and we can bury Grant honestly."

Surprise wound through Tia, and yet, she saw his logic. She recalled again his honest and fair approach with the children at the shelter. And instinctively, she knew any funeral Mac gave for a loved one would be private and dignified, respectful.

She suspected, however, if Mac had really been dead, Grant would have exploited the fact, used the funeral as a sympathy ploy, a publicity opportunity. He'd have made certain the toy's launch and his twin's interment took place on the same day.

"If not the funeral arrangements," she asked, at a loss to what he needed from her, "then what *do* you want?"

He reached for his missing beard again. "Do you suppose you could stay here?"

"With you?" An odd, unbidden warmth tightened her throat, dampened her hands.

"Separate bedrooms," he rushed to reassure her. "Of course."

"Of course," she agreed. His earnest expression was endearing. Childlike. Difficult to refuse. Despite that, she shook her head. "Look, Mac, I promise not to tell anyone that the rumors of your death are premature."

"It isn't that. It's...well...I want you to show me how to dress and talk, and whatever else I need to do to convince my employees that I *am* Grant."

He looked as though a magic wand couldn't make that happen.

So how did he expect *her* to accomplish it?

Chapter Three

"Oh, no," Tia said. "You're on your own."

Mac gaped at Tia. "How in hell am I supposed to figure out how to be Grant all by myself?"

She spread her arms, palms outward, her eyes wide as though he'd said something stupid. "Well, you're doing a pretty good job of it right now."

"What?" He glanced down at his crumpled T-shirt, at his bare feet, and his hand went automatically to his chin, gathering a fistful of bristled jaw. He jerked his hand down, but not before his ears burned. How could he unlearn a gesture he'd employed for years? "I'm wearing his clothes. I have his hairstyle. But we both know that's where the similarities end. Grant never wrinkled. Never grew whiskers. He was James frickin' Bond in the flesh. Look at me—I'm…Geppetto."

He could swear she wanted to laugh. But she shook her head, her jaw set in a stubborn tilt. "I don't want to help make you into Grant."

Mac's frustration doubled, squeezing a heavy breath from him. Didn't she know it was the only way? "Don't you understand that if I can't pull this off, the killer will murder me, too?"

"That's exactly my point." Tia's mouth went dry. Didn't he understand the danger? Even after Grant's death? No, she supposed most people couldn't conceive of bad things happening to them; their lives were untouched by true evil. She'd had the opposite experience. Twice now. She not only envisioned evil, she feared it.

She sure as hell didn't want to get grabbed by it again.

"I can't do this without you." Mac frowned, desperation issuing from his turquoise eyes. "And time is running out."

Despite her resolve to flee before the avalanche of disaster crashed down on her even harder, Tia felt it cracking the solid foundation from beneath her like ice on a pond at spring thaw. "Okay. I don't know what I can do to lend you credibility as Grant, but I'm not scheduled for another flight until next Sunday. So I'm free for the next six days, and I'll do whatever I can."

Relief snatched his frown; the change in his eyes was like sunlight hitting fresh-fallen snow. "Yes!"

As though it was an everyday thing, he swept her into an embrace, startling her. The hug had none of Grant's tried-and-tested smoothness, but sang of spontaneity, gratitude, and warmed Tia as nothing had in a very long time.

Immediately she felt Mac tense, his arms stiffening, the hug becoming an awkward clutch. Why? It was natural they would seek solace from each other in their shared grief. Before she could reassure him, Mac released her as though he'd just realized he was holding an armload of fire.

"Mac..."

Spewing apologies, the tops of his ears pink, he fled the kitchen and hurried into the living room with the speed of a man escaping some unpleasant encounter.

Tia stood riveted in place, uncertain what to think. To feel. If it was natural that they share a hug in their mutual grief over losing Grant, then what explained the guilt gnawing at her belly? And why had Mac reacted as though he also felt guilty?

Or had he? She pushed her hair away from her face. Was she misreading him, thinking because she felt disloyal he should, too? Probably. More likely he was just embarrassed.

She began loading the dishwasher. She couldn't recall ever seeing Grant embarrassed. He'd been bold and outgoing. Mac seemed shy, introverted, not normally demonstrative. The type of man who would feel extremely ill at ease whenever his feelings overwhelmed him to the point that he expressed them physically and vocally.

And yet...the image of Mac with Jonathan Tucker, a little boy whose house and all its possessions had fallen victim to the marauding Cedar River last winter, filled her mind. No one—certainly not his shell-shocked parents—had been able to draw as much as a smile from the frightened and inconsolable child. But Mac had done much more. His generous gift of new toys—none from his own company, which specialized in electronic toys—reached through the boy's stupor. Tore down his walls of resistance. That afternoon, Jonathan had laughed out loud. Tia could still hear that wonderful sound.

She found Mac in the living room. He stood with his back to her, holding himself apart as surely as if he'd erected a fence around himself. How unlike Grant he was. Opposite in every way.

This was, of course, Mac's dilemma. The very things that made him different from Grant could give him away. Get him killed.

The impact of the danger facing them froze her blood like water in a blizzard. She hugged herself against the inner chill. Lord, she had her work cut out for her. She turned on all the lights in the living room.

Mac spun around, his eyes so full of grief she felt as though she was intruding on him. She considered leaving him alone for a while, then quickly rejected the impulse. Somehow, she sensed he needed her to force this, just so he could get through it.

"We've got less than eight hours to pull off this hat trick," she said. "We'd better get started."

"Where?" He drew a shaky breath, but he seemed ready and willing, if in need of some direction.

She considered a moment. "Grant used to say the way a person walked could give him away. Walk across the room."

Mac strode toward the kitchen and back, his shoulders hunched slightly forward, his muscles taut, each step deliberate and soft. She had the odd sensation he could cross the room without stirring the air—as though he were invisible. *Or wanted to be.*

Tia cringed and shook her head as she realized he was deliberately drawing as little attention to himself as possible. Exactly the opposite of Grant. "No, no, no."

Mac stopped, eyeing her questioningly.

She circled him once, slowly, his neck twisting as he craned to watch her. She poked a finger between his shoulder blades with the same hard thrust her foster mother had used on her throughout her teens, something she'd sworn she'd never do to anyone. And even as her finger connected with his solid back, she felt infuriated at how life turned self-promises into self-prophecies.

At the jab, Mac jerked straighter, the reflexive action squaring his stance.

She smiled, nodding. "Yes, that's it. Keep those shoulders back. Grant didn't walk so much as strut. He wanted everyone to notice him when he entered a room."

And everyone usually had. The thought that someone so large in life was gone, his brilliant light snuffed out as easily as candles after Christmas mass, squeezed her heart. "Close your eyes." Her voice choked. "Picture Grant a minute, then try the walk again."

Mac did as requested, crossing the room three more times, but for all the determination on his face, strutting didn't come naturally to him. A grin tugged at the corners of her mouth. Tia never paid much attention to the way people walked, except as one noticed a limp or a drunken sway or as women noticed men's backsides.

Studying Mac now, she found the easy shift of his lean hips in his fanny-hugging jeans distracting, his graceless stride diverting because it was artless, unpracticed and infinitely male.

"I'm pathetic, right?" He stopped, frustration rife in his eyes.

"No..." She blinked, embarrassed that she'd been staring at him with God knew what expression. Her cheeks burned.

"You're a lousy liar." He made a face at her.

"No, you're improving." But even she heard the lack of conviction in her words. "Look, let's take a break, have another cup of coffee." Before he could protest, she made a beeline for the kitchen.

He arrived behind her as she was filling two clean mugs, these blue with myriad lacy snowflakes. She and Grant had not bought these together. A gift, he'd told her. From a previous girlfriend? Had he collected mugs with other women? The possibility didn't stir as much as a breath of jealousy in her, and Tia realized she hadn't really loved Grant. Not as a fiancée should.

Mac reached for one of the mugs, his hand a bit unsteady, either from weariness or grief, or perhaps a combination of both. "How am I going to convince my employees I'm not me, if I can't master Grant's persona?"

Her cup was halfway to her mouth. She lowered it, struck by a thought. Were they going about this all wrong? Aiming for an undoable, unnecessary perfection? "Maybe…just maybe, you won't need to *master* it."

"Why not?"

Her nerves pinched. "How often did Grant visit Coy Toys?"

His frown deepened, furrowing his forehead, catching in dual lines above his straight nose. A stomach-tensing moment passed while he considered.

"Once," he said finally, speaking slowly as though ticking off items on a Christmas wish list. "When I first opened the plant…then not for a long time. Maybe three more times over the past five years. Then twice this November, when he came to the lab and spoke with me and Gwen, my assistant. All other visits were after hours.''

"Then Gwen is the only one of your employees he interacted with?''

"Yes, as far as I know.''

"Good.'' Tia released a huge breath, grasping her new idea with fervor. "Good. That means in order to fool your employees you don't need to be a clone of Grant—''

"I just can't be *Mac*,'' he finished for her. He smiled crookedly, obviously finding the same relief and hope in this fact as she did. "Yeah. That should make it a lot easier.''

But it didn't. The next few hours trudged past and Mac couldn't seem to quash the habits of reaching for his beard or his glasses or his ponytail. Always he'd catch himself, drop his hand and blush. Besides that, reminding him to keep his shoulders squared and to project his voice when speaking required her constant prompting. And every time he came close to getting the walk right, or the posture, or the voice, pain shot through his expression, choked his words, undermined him.

The clock chimed five. Darkness still hugged the windows. A hopeless anxiety nipped at Tia, zapping her waning energy. He wouldn't make this on his own. Suddenly the week ahead seemed like a life sentence, a trek to the North Pole, fraught with hidden peril and a deadly, unknown menace. Any misstep could be Mac's last.

How would he maneuver the maze? Make it through alive?

She could think of only one way to improve his chances. But he wasn't going to like it. "I know you don't want me near Coy Toys, but to be brutally honest, you need me there. Right by your side.''

"What?'' Disbelief lifted his brows. "Why?''

She sighed. "To keep you from making unconscious gestures that are going to give away your true identity.''

He tensed, violently shaking his head. "No. I won't put you in danger.''

"Mac, listen to reason.''

"No.'' He raked his hand through his hair, a gesture Grant had made every day of his life, and paced the length of the room once more, his stride more assured this time, his shoulders as squared as concrete blocks. Her conviction of his shakiness faltered. Was she wrong? Could he do this without her?

He turned toward her and his hand went for his absent glasses. He stopped himself, but not before his ears glowed pink. In that moment, she saw him accept she was right.

"I guess I don't have a choice, do I?'' His voice rang with resignation.

She pressed her lips together.

"I'm a disaster as Grant.'' Anger at himself filled his words, but his face was tight with worry, lined with sorrow. "I'll be lucky to make it through today.''

"We'll make it through together.'' Wishing she felt as certain as she sounded, Tia slumped tiredly onto a corner of the sofa. Mac dropped down beside her. The shadow of his beard had darkened sometime during their long night. Perversely, it made him even handsomer. Reminded her of Grant on an early morning.

She shoved the thought, and all its accompanying confusion of grief and guilt, away. If she gave in to her sorrow now, they'd never get through the day. And they had to survive this day and the next, and the next.

Her gaze fell on the brightly wrapped package she'd left on the coffee table. She gathered it into her hand. It felt weightless in her palm, a box small enough to hold a ring.

"What did you get him?" Mac's whisper cut through her musing.

She glanced up, frowning, not understanding his question. "What?"

"Grant." He grimaced, pointing at the gift. "Do you mind telling me what you bought him?"

"I didn't get this for him. I found it out on the doorstep when I arrived last night."

His eyebrows lifted. "Who is it from?"

She shrugged. "The tag says Santa."

Mac paled.

Her pulse leaped. "What's the matter?"

"It looks like the gift *I* got from Santa."

His meaning struck home and her eyes widened. "The one with the sprig of holly berries?"

Nodding, he swallowed hard and reached for the box. Tension filled the space between them. He tore at the wrapping paper. In the silence the sound resembled the crackle-pop of a string of tree lights bursting one at a time in rapid succession.

A second later he held up a tiny box that might contain anything from a piece of jewelry to a miniature bomb. The name of his Taiwan competitor, Lei Industries, was stamped all over it. He said, "It's identical to the one I received."

"Don't open it, Mac. We don't know who sent it. Or what's in it."

He snapped his gaze from the box to her. "A mail bomb?"

"Maybe."

"I doubt it, but if it'll make you feel better." He lurched off the sofa.

She followed him to the kitchen.

"No," he said, warning her back. "Just in case you're right and I'm wrong, you should go into the foyer."

Stubbornly, every nerve tingling with fear, she retreated as far as the entrance to the kitchen and watched as he filled the sink with water, then dowsed the package. Her heart boomed in her chest, roared in her ears. It was the loudest noise in the condo.

Mac let out a huge sigh, pulled something from the water and turned to face her, holding it between his thumb and forefinger. It dripped water onto the floor at his bare feet. He pursed his lips. "We've defused a piece of paper."

Her breath heaved from her chest, burning her throat. "It looks like a ransom note, with all those crazy letters pasted on it. What does it say?"

Mac spread it on the counter. The letters, cut from various printed materials, had been glued to a piece of stationery with Coy Toys letterhead. The message was simple: *Mac Coy's death was no accident.*

He and Tia glanced at each other. Her pulse continued wobbling. "Who sent it?"

He shook his head. "I don't know. Could be from any one of my employees. Maybe even the killer."

"Why would the killer send *this* to Grant?"

"Oh, man, I don't know. I guess that doesn't make much sense. He or she sure wouldn't want Grant looking into 'my' death." Grief etched his every word, and she understood how he was struggling to stave it off. How close he was to a total meltdown. He blew out a loud breath. "God, I'm some kind of a lousy investigator. How will I ever figure out who killed Grant?"

The anguish on his face tore at her heart. "With luck you won't have to figure out who killed him."

She gathered the box and the soggy note and carried them to the living room, where she retrieved the wrapping paper and tag. "We'll turn these over to the police next week. Meanwhile, just don't voice any theories while we're at the plant. That way, no one will think we're there to do anything except get the toy out on time."

"Yes, yes." He gave her a grateful nod. "That's going to take all my concentration."

She felt ready to collapse, but the whole long day faced them. They needed a plan. "What are you going to do first this morning?"

Mac shook himself, forcing his grief back into whatever dark recess it kept springing loose from. He swallowed hard. "First thing is to call a meeting of all the staff heads and advise them that I, Grant Lee Coy, Mac Arthur Coy's twin brother and heir, am taking over the reins of the company. My first act as CEO is to move up the launch date of Holly Beary to have the bear shipped by the weekend. We can't afford to lose any of our presales, and I expect there will be a flood of calls this morning from concerned customers."

He spoke with authority and modulation, his voice sounding more like Grant's than his own. Inexplicably, a shiver crept down her spine.

"You and I will need to be there early." He

glanced at the mantel clock centered among lengths of pine swags that were anchored by red and gold candles in the shapes of the three wise men. Mac shifted his attention to her. "Do you have something to wear besides your uniform?"

"That depends on what one wears to a toy company."

"We're casual at Coy Toys. Jeans. Sweatshirt. Sweater." He pointed to his own outfit. "Anything like this."

"I have those here," she said, reminding them both of her relationship with his brother. Her cheeks warmed and she chided herself for feeling self-conscious. So what if she kept some clothes here? It wasn't as though she lived here. Besides, she didn't suppose Mac was a monk.

But he couldn't seem to look her in the eyes now. He said, "Why don't you hit the shower first?"

A shower sounded wonderful. Maybe that would warm the chill inside her. "Great."

She started for the bathroom, but pulled up short when a thought slammed into her. She pivoted, gaping at him. "Oh, my God, Mac. What were we thinking? The dress code at Coy Toys may be garage-sale chic, but Grant's idea of casual wear was chinos and a Ralph Lauren polo shirt. You're wearing one of the two pair of jeans he owns...and his only T-shirt."

"Damn, that's right." Mac rolled his eyes and his shoulders slumped as though that huge weight had settled there again. "You should have heard him grumble about how uncomfortable he felt in my work clothes. Said the cords felt as baggy as oversize sweatpants and my favorite sweatshirt should be tossed."

She watched a scowl overtake him. Pain rippled through his eyes. His jaw tensed and his Adam's apple bobbed. He pressed his lips together like a man fighting tears, hating the weakness of them, yet feeling such heartache that it controlled his nervous system, his motor responses. She realized that losing the sweatshirt was like losing an old friend, and losing his brother was like losing a vital internal organ. He could get another friend, but no amount of surgery would ever replace his missing twin.

Again the depth of his feelings for Grant awed her. Had either of them realized how lucky they were to have had each other? To know unconditional love?

Unexpectedly Mac chuckled, a sad little sound, bursting with affection. ''Grant said the only way he'd be able to tolerate the discomfort was by thinking of the outfit as a costume.''

Tia offered him a melancholy smile. She could hardly imagine Grant in baggy cords and a ratty old sweatshirt. But she'd bet Mac would feel just as ill-outfitted in Grant's favorite Armani suit. Which was what he'd be wearing in an hour or so.

''I SWEAR THIS NECKTIE is strangling me.'' Mac tugged at the collar of his dress shirt. ''I don't know how Grant could breathe in this getup everyday.''

The street light turned green, a color as brilliant as Tia's eyes. He lifted his foot off the clutch, jammed his other onto the gas pedal. The Porsche lurched forward in a jerking motion like a remote-control car being operated by a child. Tia bounced in the seat beside him, but said nothing.

Mac swore under his breath. Grant's shoes—some Italian designer's version of suede loafers—were new, the soles slick, the fit too loose. Too uncomfortable. Too much of a reminder that he could never fill his brother's shoes.

Tia stared out the window, but he suspected her attention was turned inward. Her silence punctuated his loneliness. He swallowed hard, grappling for control of his grief with every ounce of will he could muster. *Think of something else. Anything else.*

He slowed for another light, downshifting. The sky was still dark, heavy commuter traffic still a good ten minutes away from hitting the roads, his employees still at home, grabbing that last-minute cup of coffee before starting for work. He considered the deception Tia and he would perpetrate this morning, and all week, on those people, people he had once trusted implicitly, most of whom deserved his trust and respect—who didn't deserve to be used as he must use them now.

What consequences would his actions earn?

This mental path led him straight back to Grant and his own trepidation about entering the place where his brother had died, a place that he, Mac, had built with love and expectation, a place he'd wanted to stand for all that was good in the world of business. He'd been a fool to think such a thing was possible. Once again the betrayal twisted his gut, coming at him like a drunk driver suddenly in his lane, crashing headlong into him, smashing his trust and faith like so much buckled metal and broken glass.

He'd hired the Judas, invited the snake into his Garden of Eden. That mistake, that lapse in judgment, had cost him his brother.

Anger climbed his neck and made the damnable collar seem two sizes smaller. Fury was alien to him.

Mac Coy didn't get mad. He was known for his slow fuse. Hell, he didn't even raise his voice or speak in anger. But he was angry now. And he couldn't seem to shake it. He jammed his foot to the floor, sending the car rushing ahead as he steered around a slow-moving van.

"Well." Tia broke the silence. "Whatever else you haven't gotten down pat, you can rest assured you're driving like Grant."

He glanced toward her, her dark hair shiny in the glow of the headlights behind them. "I'm sorry. I'm...I'm so furious I could hit something. I can't remember ever feeling this way. I can't talk myself down. Can't shake it off."

She faced him, her expression resigned. "Maybe you shouldn't try."

"Why not?"

"Because it isn't going to go away, so you may as well put it to use."

She sounded as though she was talking from experience, and he realized he knew very little about this woman who owned his disloyal heart. And with his lack of social skills, he wasn't likely to find out much. What did it matter, really? He could never claim Tia as his own. His ire spiked a notch higher. "How exactly do I put this anger to good use?"

"By not letting it go. It will give you an edginess that will make you appear more like Grant and less like yourself to those you've worked with for years."

Again he had the impression she spoke from experience. He wondered what in her life had made her as angry as this. He didn't ask. Her past was none of his business, nor would it affect him in any way. Besides, time had run out. "The plant is just down this road."

He pulled into a private lane. They had reached the area above Renton called May Valley, a ten-minute drive from Grant's condo in Kennydale.

Tia asked, "Don't you live around here somewhere?"

He pointed along the road they'd just left. "Half a mile or so east."

He pulled up to the gate and glanced at the three-story building behind the eight-foot chain-link fence. It was as oblong as a child's toy box, but more resembled a giant igloo without the domed top. This time of year it always reminded him of a Christmas cake. The purple and gold stripes across the top section of the structure were like narrow ribbons of candy, the purple window frames like sugar plums stuck in white frosting.

How could anyone have died here? Committed murder here? Mac swiped his card key through the electronic guard. The gates moved open with a soft whir. He drove through, circled to the back of the building and parked before a solid-looking purple door in a spot marked Reserved.

Only one other car stood nearby. He told Tia, "The night watchman is here somewhere, but otherwise, we're the first to arrive. Come on. We're using my entrance."

He ushered her into his private elevator and they ascended to the third-floor landing. The hall was well-lit, but eerily silent in the absence of his staff. He'd often worked late and never before noticed or minded the quiet. It seemed alive, dangerous, this morning.

"Over here." He directed her toward the end of

the hallway. Once they were inside, he turned on the lights and shut the door.

The blinds were drawn. The large room had the appearance of a combination conference and storage room. Floor-to-ceiling shelves lined two walls to their left, each crammed with enough toys to fill Santa's bag three times over. He'd personally decorated the tree near the windows. Christmas had always been his favorite time of year. Would it ever be again?

A computer, scanner and printer claimed a massive mahogany desk to their right, and in the center of the room stood an oblong table surrounded by half a dozen chairs. All disks and important data were locked in the safe in the closet beyond.

Mac strode to the desk. His emotions boiled again, roiling into a mass of anger and grief, weighing heavy on his spirit. ''Well, this is it—my office.''

''Hello, Mac.'' The voice that came from behind him was not Tia's.

Mac froze, shock charging through him like a jolt of electricity. The Porsche keys slipped from his hand and clattered to the hardwood floor. Dear God, no! He'd worried about making it through the day as Grant. He hadn't made it through ten minutes. Whoever had killed his twin was about to murder again.

With his heart climbing his throat, he turned to face his adversary.

Chapter Four

The look of horror on Mac's face echoed the fear swelling in Tia. She lurched around. Her pulse rang in her ears. Every nerve in her body twitched. But Mac and she were alone in the room. She gaped at him, frowning. "What was it? An intercom...or something?"

Mac shook his head, his eyes wide. "I don't kn—"

"Don't be afraid, Mac." The voice said again. "You aren't alone."

Tia jolted. She glanced at the shelves of toys from where the voice emanated, then questioningly at Mac. A sheepish grin was spreading across his face.

Relief shifted through her with such force her knees wobbled. "A toy?"

"Not just any toy." He crossed the room and reached for a fluffy, snow white teddy bear no larger than a newborn baby, perched on a middle shelf, its arms outstretched as though waiting for him. He held it up for her to see. It had huge, gold-flecked onyx eyes that seemed to follow her as she moved closer. The inside of the ears were red velvet, as were the bear's nose and mittens. A sprig of holly berries hugged its neck.

"Meet Holly Beary," he said with affection and pride. "This is the prototype."

"I love you, Mac," the bear replied.

Tia was impressed. She feathered her fingers across the teddy's head. "It has such a sweet face, and is so soft. Is it voice-activated?"

"Yes, but there's more to Holly than that. Her 'heart' is the real magic of the toy." He plunged his fingers into the bear's chest and a second later withdrew them, holding what appeared to be a small, heart-shaped bit of red plastic, no larger than two inches long or wide, between his forefinger and thumb. "The technology on this microchip is what makes her so extraordinarily special."

"How so?"

"As you've observed, she isn't just voice-activated, she's voice-sensitive. She speaks only when *I* speak. She's been programmed to answer my voice alone."

Tia began to understand.

"And it can be programmed to anyone's voice?"

"Yes. That's the wonderful thing. With this, kids the world over can now own a teddy bear who responds to them like a real friend, addressing them by name and speaking only when *they* speak to her. There are eighteen preprogrammed responses. The microchip decides which one to use by the tone of the voice it's programmed to answer."

"A sad child, a sad response?" she asked.

He shook his head. "A sad child, a loving response."

She beamed at him. "Even better."

"Yeah, I know. It's the perfect toy for an only child."

"For any *lonely* child." *I could have used one of these.* She could have used anything that would have eased the sadness she'd lived with, the sense of being unloved, unwanted. "Better than an invisible friend."

"Much." He pushed the microchip heart partially back into the bear and set the toy on the worktable. "But that's just one of the many features—like movement sensitivity. See her eyes follow as I move my hand?"

"That's amazing. And wonderful. How...?"

Mac blinked at her, wonder slipping into his expression as he realized she was really interested in what he'd done to make this toy a reality. His eyebrows flickered and he cocked his head. "Do you understand computer science or technology?"

Tia shook her head. "Not a lick."

He grinned, a small, self-deprecating lift of the corners of his mouth. "It's a subject I could talk about for hours, but since you'd likely begin staring at me with glazed eyes after five minutes..."

"Okay." She tilted her head and lifted a strand of hair from her cheek. "Then, where did the idea come from?"

He blew out a quiet breath. "From a dream. I was about eight the first time I had that dream. I had to wait twenty years for present-day technology to catch up to my vision."

"It's a gem." She fingered the bear again. What must it feel like to do something so well that it could change another person's world for the better? She couldn't even guess. "I can only imagine how much work has gone into it."

"Three long years. Incalculable number of twelve-hour days. Umpteen all-nighters. Not to mention every penny I could lay hold of just to develop this prototype. But I'd do it all again.'' Gratification shone in his eyes. ''The result exceeded even my expectations.''

''I can see now why Grant wanted this toy launched on schedule as much as you do.''

The sorrow hovering like an aura around him settled in his expression again, and Tia ached to help ease his pain, to ease her own misery over their shared loss. But how? Nothing she could say or do would resurrect Grant.

''What I want—'' his voice broke ''—is for this toy to be affordable, so that every kid can have one. If it was up to me, I'd give the bears away.''

Recalling his generosity with the children at the shelter, Tia knew he spoke the truth. Mac would rather wear ratty old sweatshirts than Armani suits, scuffed tennis shoes than Italian loafers—if it meant a child would not have to go without a toy. He'd spent his income on the children of strangers. His generosity humbled her, and she wondered if it extended to all aspects of his personality. Was he also a generous lover?

Heat shivered through her, delicious, unbidden and inappropriate. She swallowed against her appraisal, berated herself for such wayward thoughts, but she couldn't help envying any woman lucky enough to earn his affection.

He ran his hand across the top of his hair. ''My accountant keeps reminding me, however, that Coy Toys, Inc. is on the verge of bankruptcy. Holly Beary is our only hope for a future.''

As he spoke she watched his eyes darken, saw the lines around his mouth pinch, heard the dull ache of sorrow in his voice. It was bad enough he had a thieving employee who might cost him his lifework—she understood that hell only too well. But Mac's thief had taken something even more precious: Grant.

Her heart hitched and tears burned her eyes. Her hand began lifting toward him before she realized and stopped herself. But the yearning to comfort him nearly overwhelmed her, and she discovered with a jolt that what she felt for Mac went deeper than anything she'd ever felt for Grant. Her face flamed. How had she nearly married a man who didn't touch her soul as this man did? How had she slept with him? Planned a future with him?

And what right did she have spinning impossible dreams about Mac? Nothing had changed.

Tia hugged herself. She would not fall in love with Mac Coy—no matter how right it felt.

Mac hit the top of the desk and swore. ''God, the precautions I took—guarding the toy and its precious microchip as if they were gold in Fort Knox. My mistake was in trying to keep the spies out. When all the while, the spy was already on the inside.''

''Mac, shouldn't we go and check out the VR simulator before your employees start arriving?''

Her suggestion eclipsed his outburst. He glanced at the clock, then rounded on her, his eyes wide. ''Yes. It *is* getting late.''

''We'd better hurry, then.'' She started for the door ahead of him. But before they reached it, a rangy man with blazing red hair on his head and chin burst in. His eyes were narrowed, his expression alert, suspicious. His hand rode the gun at his hip.

Tia drew back, startled.

"Who are you?" he growled at her. "How'd you get up here?"

A hint of recognition struggled upward through her fear-fogged brain.

"I'm Grant Coy," Mac said, stepping into the man's line of vision. "The new owner of this plant."

The redhead reared back, gasping as if he'd seen a ghost. Tia supposed he probably thought he had.

Mac said, "I think you'd better tell us who you are and what you're doing with that gun. My brother was a gun-control advocate."

Tia's muscles eased at Mac's quick thinking. She wouldn't have been at all surprised if he'd forgotten that he wasn't supposed to know exactly who this man was or why he was here.

"Well, sure. I know who you are." The man's head did a slow bob. He released hold of his gun and offered a hand to Mac. Mac ignored it. Probably afraid he'd give himself away, Tia thought. His aloofness reminded her of Grant. "We spoke on the phone yesterday. I'm the security guard. Bud Gibson."

"Buddy?" Tia gaped at the redheaded man, recognition hitting her. Ginny's kid brother—the youngest of the three bad seeds. She hadn't seen him in years. Last she'd heard, he was doing one to five on a felony conviction. The hair at her nape bristled. Putting Bud Gibson in charge of security was like handing Al Capone the keys to Alcatraz. Why hadn't Ginny told her he was working for Coy Toys?

"Tia?" Bud's widening gaze rolled over her. He hadn't recognized her, either, apparently. "What are *you* doing here?"

"Ms. Larken is my fiancée," Mac answered, but

curiosity swam in his eyes. "You two know each other?"

"Buddy, er, Bud is the brother of my best friend," she explained. "I didn't realize he worked for Mac."

Bud glanced at Tia, noticing the huge diamond on her finger. A gleam entered his eyes, and she knew if he could have he'd have stripped the ring from her finger or the jewel from its setting with that look. He offered her a broad grin, showing off large, even, cigarette-stained teeth. "You've come up in the world, T. Congratulations."

"Thank you." Tia's pulse wobbled. Apparently Ginny hadn't told Buddy anything about her life, either. She supposed she ought to be grateful. But recalling her friend's distress the past week and the alarm and fear she'd seen in Ginny's eyes when they'd learned of Mac's death sent acid through her stomach. For her friend's sake, Tia prayed Buddy wasn't Mac's thief. Grant's killer.

"And the gun?" Mac insisted. "What are you doing with it?"

"Mac—er, your brother instigated a new policy two days ago. He directed me and Ford, the daytime guard, to start wearing them while on duty."

"I see." Mac didn't like this. He hated guns with a passion; however, he supposed Grant had had good reason to worry. But the guns hadn't saved him or Holly Beary. "I'm changing that order back to the original, Gibson. I don't want anyone getting shot accidentally. So leave that thing at home when you go today and inform Ford of the same."

"Sure thing. And if there's anything I can do for you, Mr. Coy..."

"Actually there is. You aren't off duty soon, are you?"

"I'm on another hour."

"Good. When the staff arrives, tell them I'd like them all to gather in here for a meeting."

"Sure thing." Bud crossed to the window and opened the blinds. The dark sky had given way to a gray dawn. He glanced out the window, then back at Mac. "Ms. Rice is just pulling in now. She's the office manager and your brother's personal secretary and assistant."

Mac stiffened. "Go let her in and relay my message about the staff meeting. Ms. Larken and I have something to attend to before everyone arrives."

Bud hurried out and a moment later they heard the main elevator descending. Mac caught Tia by the arm. "Come on. The simulator is on the second floor. We'll take the stairs."

The second-floor landing was a twin to the third, long and wide with four closed doors on the side opposite the elevator. Mac led Tia to a room at the end of the hall. It was directly below his office, but was little more than a large walk-in closet. He'd steeled himself for this, uncertain he could face the place his brother died. Or the weapon that had killed him.

It was the real reason he hadn't come to check it out last night. But he'd put it off long enough. He had to do this. Sweat beaded his upper lip. He shoved the door open and hit the switch. Brilliant illumination flooded the room, highlighting the armchair with its back to him. His breath caught at the sight of the scorched headrest. His brother had died here in that chair. *Don't dwell on that.* He started toward the chair, his steps hitched as though he were a puppet with shortened leg strings.

Tia hung back in the doorway.

Mac rounded the chair and swore. "It's not here."

"What?"

"The simulator. It should be on this chair. Or in this room." His gaze flew from corner to corner. It wasn't here. He felt all hope of catching his brother's killer dissolving like icicles from a sun-drowned ski-lodge roof. "Someone removed it on purpose."

"Who?" She frowned. "The police?"

"Why would they take it? Bud told me last night they'd declared Grant's death an accident. Frayed cord. All they were going to do was file a report for Labor and Industries."

"Maybe Bud took the simulator."

Her suggestion surprised Mac. What didn't he know about Bud Gibson? "I'll ask him, but I think our killer took it."

"Are you so sure Bud didn't kill Grant?"

He strode toward her, more confused and curious than ever. "You know him better than I do. What do you think?"

She blushed and shook her head. "I wouldn't want it to be Buddy."

"Yeah, well he's as likely a suspect as the rest right now. The only one I don't suspect is you."

Tia's face was as gray as the morning. He longed to stroke her silken cheek, just a touch to erase the stricken pallor from her skin. He held his hand rigid at his side, fighting off his own distress. His own sense of helplessness.

He'd figured on handing that simulator over to the police next week. It would help prove his claims that

Grant was murdered. Now he feared there might never be any proof. Rage and frustration collided in his head, banging together like irate reindeer bucks.

"Does this change any of your plans for the toy's launch?" Tia asked.

He thought about that a moment, then shook his head. "No. It just makes me more determined than ever to catch the rat in my woodpile."

She gave him a smile of approval. "All right, then. I suppose we'd better get back to your office. The staff should be assembling by now."

He let out a loud breath. "Okay. I can't put this off forever." But he was rattled. Without thinking he reached for Tia's elbow. The second he realized it, he started to pull back. But she caught his hand and held on tight.

He gazed down at her, noticing her skin was still a touch too pale. He cursed himself for not realizing the effect that seeing where Grant died might have on her. She'd put on a brave facade, thus far going every extra mile he'd asked of her. Even this gruesome one. She wanted Grant's killer caught as much as he did. The depth of her commitment to his twin gladdened him, and filled him with such envy he ached with self-loathing.

In the elevator she relinquished her hold on him. Mac's arm chilled as though her touch had been all that was keeping him warm. She studied him, straightening his jacket and tie, brushing a speck of lint from his lapel, the way a wife might do for her husband before an important job interview. The intimacy thickened his throat, and his need for her to be more than a friend speared him. He stepped back from her.

She seemed not to notice his discomposure, nodding, instead, in satisfaction. "There, that's better. Are you ready?"

To face his staff as Grant? Was he? "I guess we'll find out in a minute."

The elevator doors swung open. Nancy Rice stood there as though she'd been waiting for them. Her eyes widened slightly at the sight of Mac, and her breath seemed to hitch. She recovered quickly. "I'm Nancy Rice, Mr. Coy. Your brother's personal assistant." A shapely brown-eyed blonde, Nancy wore her usual outfit, a brightly colored spandex top and skin-tight jeans.

Mac introduced Tia, but Nancy gave her short shrift, acknowledging her only with a polite nod of her head. Her attention kept returning to him. Had he somehow given himself away? His mouth dried. He shifted uncomfortably, scowling at her. "Is something wrong, Ms. Rice?"

"No, nothing. Excuse me for staring. It was such a shock last week when Mac decided to shave and cut his hair. I was just getting used to his new look, and now, seeing you, it's rather jarring, you know?" Her round eyes filled with tears.

Two weeks ago Mac would have thought her sorrow genuine. Now he didn't know. Didn't know who in his employ was honest and who was acting. He hated that and it roused his ire. An odd sense of strength reared up in him, making a shield between himself and this woman's feelings.

For the first time in his life he felt insensitive to another's suffering, to the grief shown by a woman he'd known and worked closely with for many years.

Was this how Tia had meant for him to use his anger?

Mac nodded toward his closed office door. "Is the staff assembled?"

"Yes, but before we go in, I was hoping…well, it might be impertinent of me, but given my close professional relationship with Mac, well, I…the truth is, Mr. Coy, we're all a little concerned about this meeting. About your plans for the future of Coy Toys."

Mac nodded and started forward. "I intend to discuss that with you all. Meanwhile, Ms. Larken is going to be acting as my assistant. No offense, Ms. Rice, but I'm used to her help and I would appreciate your full cooperation this week in particular."

Nancy Rice's face paled. "Does this mean that I'll soon be looking for another job?"

"That will depend on Holly Beary," he said cryptically. The less time he spent sparring with Nancy the better. Of all his employees, she scared him the most. Not because she might be the murderer—although that was a concern—but because she knew Mac Coy better than the others. He opened the office door, gesturing for the women to proceed him.

Stand straight. Speak loudly. Don't touch your nose, he instructed himself. Still, he feared he'd give himself away. He held his body rigid and entered his office.

Five minutes later the meeting was over, his department heads filing out. He'd kept it simple, assuring all that their jobs were not in jeopardy—as long as they could get Holly Beary ready for shipment by the weekend.

Even as he said this, he knew one of them would

not be pleased, but for the life of him, he couldn't tell which.

Before anyone could protest the increased work-load, he outlined exactly how he expected them to carry it off, showing them it was not impossible if they concentrated on their own part of the toy's assemblage.

Finally, forestalling an endless stream of questions, he assured them all he'd come and talk with each individually sometime during the day. Meanwhile, there was no time to waste. His dismissal had them looking a bit unsure, glancing at Nancy for support as they shifted up and out of their chairs and began filing out of the office, mumbling amongst themselves.

Mac stopped Nancy at the door. "Ms. Rice, I'd appreciate it if you'd personally handle the phones. There's likely to be press calling and, more importantly, worried customers. Please assure them all that Coy Toys, Inc. is carrying on as my brother would have wanted. Holly Beary will be delivered as promised."

"Please, call me Nancy, Grant." There was a new gleam in her lovely brown eyes, an invitation he'd never seen or been offered before. Nancy was flirting with him. The realization zinged through Mac, spoke to the deepest male part of him. His pleasure in how he'd handled the meeting skewed, lapsing like a forgotten license. Women never flirted with him.

He didn't seek or encourage advances. He'd humiliated himself to the core the two times he'd had sexual encounters—both blind dates set up for him by Grant. Heat seared his insides at the embarrassing memories. "Fastest gun in the west," the first woman had laughingly called him. But she hadn't thought it funny when he couldn't "reload his weapon" after she'd stopped giggling. The second woman hadn't been that kind. Had either or both of them told Grant?

He shook himself, feeling the heat climb to his ears. He was better off without romantic entanglements. Besides, living like a monk wasn't all bad. It gave him plenty of time to work. Not to mention an appreciation for the therapy of cold showers.

And yet, the soft come-on in Nancy's eyes sent a strange, not unwelcome sensation fluttering through him. He felt a sappy grin sliding across his face. Felt powerless to stop it.

Tia did that. "Thank you, *Nancy*. I think Grant would appreciate it if you got busy now."

Nancy gave her a polite but chilly nod of the head and left them alone. Tia shut the door, then stood leaning against it, staring at him. She and Nancy were like day and night. Nancy's sexuality was as glaring as the sun, obvious and overwhelming, whereas Tia's was as gentle and intriguing as the moon.

He was male. His body responded to both women, but he wouldn't overstep propriety with either of them. Nancy didn't interest him, and Tia deserved better than a bungler. Besides, she had loved his brother. Loved him still.

He realized she was glaring at him. Distress arrowed through him. "What? Did I do something wrong? Give myself away?"

Her silent reprimand fled her glorious eyes and she seemed almost embarrassed. She blinked. Squared her slender shoulders. "No, in fact, you were great. I think they were all impressed."

"Not all. One of them wants me dead."

Tia hugged herself as if against a sudden chill. "Would that really be necessary when they could throw you off by simply seeing—instead—that you don't make the launch date?"

The possibility riveted him. He felt like a man whose Christmas tree had burned down his house, robbing him of all the joy that should have accompanied the holiday celebration, stealing his every possession and layering him with the ash of distrust.

Betrayal. Murder. And now, sabotage?

Chapter Five

"Grant wanted me to install hidden video cameras in all of my managers' offices and in the work areas." Mac swiped his face with his hands, looking torn, disgusted with himself.

Tia perched a hip on the corner of the conference table. She understood feeling guilty for something you hadn't done. But wishing it different didn't make it so. "Is it too late to do that now?"

"I won't do it. The idea of spying on my employees—" he broke off, shaking his head.

And she realized she'd misread the source of his disgust. He didn't hate himself, he detested the situation and the idea that violating his people's privacy was the only way to make it right.

"If I'd listened to Grant, we probably would have found the traitor straightaway."

And Grant would likely still be alive.

Neither said it, but Tia knew he shared the thought, just as he shared the sorrow blooming within her. Her heart reached out to him, and she ached to ease his pain. "Grant always believed in fighting fire with fire."

"I know, but doing something unethical even to

catch a criminal goes against everything *I* believe in. How would you feel if you found out after the fact you'd been spied on by your employer?''

''I don't think I'd like it.'' She would hate it.

''You see what I mean?'' He waved his hands in frustration. ''I have to work with these people after the betrayer is caught. But if I treat them all like they're guilty, then how many of them will still want to work with me?''

She couldn't imagine any of them not wanting to work with Mac. He was a fair and generous man. Surely he was that kind of employer. On the other hand, she'd had her share of lousy bosses. If she discovered she'd been videotaped at work without her knowledge, her trust would be stripped away. Would she stay with such a company? Even if they had legitimate reasons for their action? Not after her experience with Crimble Industries. Not after knowing one picture could override a thousand declarations of innocence.

She laid her hand over Mac's, finding strength in the warm encounter—and a frisson of guilty pleasure that had her releasing him as quickly as she'd reached for him. What was the matter with her? Allowing herself to forget, wanting something she couldn't have? She lifted the offending hand self-consciously through her hair, warding off a wave of despair. ''You know, we could go on all day discussing coulda, shoulda, wouldas. But we can't go back and change things. So, how do we assure that Holly Beary gets launched without a hitch?''

Mac rubbed his forefinger under his lower lip, a gesture belonging wholly to Mac. She worried anew whether or not they could pull off this charade.

He tipped his head to the side, his expression serious. "In lieu of being flies on the wall, I guess we'll have to police things as best we can. But we can't be everywhere at once."

"Agreed. But we have to do something."

He thought a moment. "I told the department heads I'd pay them each a visit today. Since neither of us is supposed to know the first thing about the toy business, I guess it won't seem odd if we ask a lot of questions about what they're doing."

Tia scooted off the table. The department heads. Mac's first line of suspects, one of whom had probably killed Grant. And now they were going one on one, face-to-face with each of them. The prospect was daunting. What if Mac gave himself away? Somehow alerted the wrong person to the fatal mistake he or she had made?

The urge to call this whole sham to a halt swept over her. She'd agreed to help Mac get his Christmas toy launched. Not to find a killer. Belatedly she was realizing the two things went hand in hand. Fear skittered through her, but she managed to keep it from her face. She just couldn't get cold feet now. Mac needed her. She forced a confident smile. "So, where do we start, 'Grant'?"

He straightened his spine, squared his shoulders and executed that forefinger-and-thumb, pistol-shooting-at-you gesture Grant always used, instead of saying, "sure thing," or, "okay." The simple pantomime lacked Grant's grace, looked awkward. Tia's sense of impending disaster deepened.

Mac opened the door. "Might as well start at the bottom and work our way up."

Short minutes later the elevator deposited them in

a huge warehouse area with roll-up doors hanging open to the cold December air. The area teemed with voices and machinery, the commotion of a bustling team scrambling toward a singular goal.

In a low voice Mac explained that this part of the building was divided into two sections, each as long as the structure. He leaned toward her as he spoke, his warm breath feathering against her ear, her cheek. She swayed unwittingly closer to him.

He said, "This is shipping and receiving."

Rubbing her outer arms with both hands, Tia wrestled with the pleasant sensation his nearness stirred, but she couldn't stifle the yearning deep inside her—that needy, empty hole in her heart that responded to this man as it had to no other.

Beneath the tug of attraction, however, tension knotted her stomach. Nervously, she eyed the freight truck hugging the nearest bay. A man on a hydraulic forklift was pulling boxes from within its depths, then delivering them to a growing mound near the elevator. She watched for some sort of response to "Grant," but the man ignored them.

"Empty." Mac told her, pointing to the cartons. "They're filling them in Marketing."

Tia spotted a counter at the far end wall. A man with a phone to his ear was staring at them intently. Despite the cold, sweat beaded her upper lip. "Is that the shipping clerk? Are we going to speak with him first?"

Mac gave a short, nervous chortle.

"What?" She stiffened, befuddled.

"That's Fred Vogler, the operations manager." Mac relaxed a modicum, a teasing glint lighting his turquoise eyes. The warm gleam sent a honeyed shiver through her. "He's responsible for getting the toys shipped to our customers. He'd be highly offended at being called a clerk."

"Oh." She swept her hair behind one ear, her hand shaky. "I guess my naïveté is a plus, but if anyone catches you talking with such authority about the running of this company..."

He winced and his ears reddened. "I'll remember."

She prayed he would, because at the moment, he loped beside her in an easy gait that was nothing like Grant's strut. She glanced sharply in all directions to see if anyone had noticed. Fred Vogler was still staring at them. Her stomach clutched. She had to warn Mac.

As she moved toward him, she spotted an approaching employee. He, too, was frowning at Mac. Her throat tightened. She grasped Mac's arm and pulled him close against her. She felt his indrawn breath as his upper arm connected with her breast, felt an echoing disturbance in her very depths. Heat coiled in her, brushed her face. She whispered, "Grant, darling, you're walking like Mac."

The employee, a rangy young man with blond, shoulder-length dreadlocks bouncing on his head, matched the stiff grin Tia gave him. He wore a ring in his nose, a padded vest over a quilted flannel shirt, logger socks and boots, and, in spite of the cold, calf-length jeans. His blue eyes widened as he took in Mac. "Whoa, dude. You could *be* Mac."

"Well, I'm not," Mac assured him in his best Grant voice.

"I know, dude." The man nodded his head. "That'd be impossible, wouldn't it?"

But his gaze narrowed at Mac as though he questioned the truth of his own statement.

Tia's mouth dried, her body flushing damply.

Mac growled, "I'm *Grant* Coy. Who are you?"

"Stewart Stewicki, but everybody calls me Stewy. I work in shipping."

"Then I suggest you get on with whatever you're doing."

Stewy hesitated, and Tia's pulse jumped. Had he realized this was Mac? Or was the guy just worrying about his job and the future of Coy Toys with this "dude" at the helm?

"What don't you understand about getting back to work, Stewy?" Mac asked in a deceptively soft tone. "I presume you know by now the launch has been moved up?"

"Yep." Stewy nodded, his hair jumping. "I just wanted, well, to say I'm sorry about your brother, dude."

Mac's frown softened. "Thank you."

Stewy nodded again. "Man, what an ugly way to die."

Mac paled. Stewy's eyebrows shot up and he looked as though he'd like to reel his words back in, but at least he didn't compound the faux pas by trying to apologize or explain it. "You here to see Fred, er, Mr. Vogler?"

"No." Mac straightened his tie, and his composure. "No, I want to see Suzanne…Ms. Chang."

Stewy pointed along the wall. "She's down there, getting the temps online. And checking the new arrivals."

Temps? New arrivals? Tia's breath snagged. Again she scanned the warehouse. Was anyone else watching them? No. Even Vogler had spun the other way now. But what about these new people? An even worse thought struck her. What if one of them knew Grant? "What temps?"

Stewy shrugged. "We always hire temporary workers when we have an order this size going out. They make up the assembly line."

"I see." She saw nothing. What assembly line? She patted her arms, the cold fear clammy inside her.

"I guess we have a lot to learn," Mac added.

"Hey, I could help you out, dude," Stewy offered. "You know, show you around the plant."

"Thanks, but I think we'll just take it as it comes." Mac shook his head, then gently reminded Stewy, "I'm sure you're needed elsewhere."

"Oh, yeah, right on, dude." Stewy had the grace to look sheepish. He bobbed his dreadlocks at them one more time, then ambled off toward the rest rooms.

Mac caught Tia's clammy hand in both of his dry ones. Apparently he wasn't as uptight as she'd thought he was. Or else he was hiding it better. Her fingers nuzzled his palm as though with a will of their own. Her quavery stomach calmed, and warmth hurried the chill from her blood. His touch felt right and good.

He squinted at her, dipping his head lower. "I should have suggested you bring your coat. You're freezing."

"No, just anxious." The right, good feeling slipped into guilty pleasure. She knew she should pull free, but couldn't. "I always get cold when I'm nervous."

He squeezed her hand, the pressure reassuring and sensual at the same time. She struggled with the lonely ache inside. As right as his touch seemed to her, she was not right for Mac. For his sake, she couldn't encourage that tender gleam in his eyes.

Now she did pull free. Abruptly. Mac looked relieved, and somehow that hurt worst of all.

"That's Suzanne over there." He pointed. "The one buried in the boxes of new arrivals."

"New arrivals?" Confusion chased off Tia's personal concerns. "I thought the temps and the new arrivals were one and the same."

Mac laughed again, and again it was short and rife with hidden nerves. "Hardly, but I'll let Suzanne explain that to you...er, to us."

He steered her along the dividing wall toward a conveyor belt that emerged from a pass-through opening in the partition and disappeared into a similar opening farther on, forming a giant C.

She watched workers at the far end load the fluffy white bears face up on the moving belt. The toys moved slowly through the opening and disappeared. Oblong packages wrapped in cellophane emerged from the opening at this end. Tucked inside each was a single Holly Beary, her snowball-fat cheeks and red velvet nose pressed against the clear wrapping like a child peering into a candy shop.

She swept an apprehensive gaze across the two women stacking the packages into the master carton. But neither gave Mac or her a second look. Still she felt uneasy. Watched. She scanned the warehouse, but found nothing to explain the sensation. No one appeared to be paying attention to them. Workers *did* glance at "Grant" as they passed, but mostly she detected sadness and pity in their faces. Not suspicion.

They headed for Suzanne. A petite woman in a sweatshirt twice her size, she was bent over an open carton. She seemed to be doing a quality check on the bears before handing them along for transport on the conveyor belt.

"Ms. Chang," Mac called out.

Suzanne started, her spine tensing as though his voice had cut through her shoulder blades. She jerked around, her gaze flying to him. Something as dark as distress danced across her tiny face, and something less definable. Tia froze. Fear crashed through her. But Suzanne shook off the momentary upset before Tia could discern its source. Sorrow? Or guilt?

"Something wrong with the bears?" Mac's Adam's apple bobbed.

Tia recalled from the meeting earlier that Suzanne was head of product marketing—although what her job entailed remained a mystery. Apparently, quality control of some sort.

"Oh, no. Top quality, as always." Suzanne's delicate mouth tipped up at the corners, but the pride went all the way to her intelligent dark brown eyes.

"Good." Mac kept his voice deep and strong, hiding his relief well.

They could not afford any disasters if the launch was to go as scheduled. But she and Mac both knew that preventing them would likely prove impossible.

"Why don't we talk in my office?" Suzanne stepped toward them on feet that looked too small to carry a grown woman. Short raven hair capped her face, accentuating her almond-shaped eyes. Energy arced from her like a hyper-hum in the air.

They followed Suzanne through a door next to the end of the conveyor belt. "Product Marketing" was painted in black lettering on the glass inset. Warmer air brushed Tia's cheeks, chasing some of the chill from her limbs. On this side of the wall the conveyor belt formed a much wider C. The bears rode the belt past a line of workers performing various tasks. Some were plugging the heart-shaped computer chips into the toy's chest, while others were inserting the bears into their packaging. Once that was done, the package rolled through a machine and came out the other end in cellophane wrapping.

Workers glanced at ''Grant'' and her. Tia held her breath. But she saw nothing more than the sadness and pity she'd detected in other employees. She blew out the breath through clenched teeth.

Suzanne said, ''As assembly lines go, it's a crude setup by some standards, I suppose. But Mac insisted on the personal touch for this toy. Plus, it kept the cost down. It's less expensive to hire temporary workers than to purchase the machines that insert the computer chips and stuff the bears into the packages. And I think you'll appreciate that the toy must be affordable to be profitable.''

''Definitely,'' Mac said.

With a start Tia realized he held himself as stiff as one of the cartons in the warehouse. Anxiety stirred the acid in her belly. What if he keeled over? She hoped he hadn't locked his knees. She'd seen grown men black out at weddings from that very ploy against nerves.

Suzanne gestured toward her office at the back. Her desk faced plate-glass windows that overlooked the assembly line. There was no window to the outside. A built-in counter, with cupboards beneath, embraced the other three walls. Above two of the counters, cork boards, framed in oak, sported scraps of fabric and drawings and color renderings of Holly Beary from her earliest conception to the finished product, and the last counter held three cutaway models of the bear.

Obviously Suzanne's job comprised more than quality control.

Awed fascination snagged Tia's attention as she moved from drawing to drawing. It was like looking at someone's baby pictures, at the different stages of growth. She was so caught up in her perusal, it took her a few minutes to realize that Mac hadn't given the pictures more than a brief glance. He wasn't looking at these as though seeing them for the first time—as he should have been.

Her heart fell to her toes. She had to warn him. Get him back on track. But how? She took a step toward him. Then stopped herself. He wasn't standing wrong. He wasn't rubbing his chin or poking his missing glasses up the bridge of his nose. So what was it? Something odd. He kept shifting his gaze from corner to corner as though assessing the room and its contents and finding them lacking.

Relief shuddered through Tia. Contrary to what she'd been thinking, Mac was doing a great job imitating his twin. Grant wouldn't have given the drawings more than a cursory once-over, either. He'd never cared about how a thing came into being, about what made it work. He found no interest in dreaming and seeing a dream reach fruition.

Grant preferred knowing what made people tick. Why they did the things they did. It was this curiosity that brought him success as a detective.

Suzanne, however, didn't seem to like Mac's uninterested attitude. She pointed at the wall as though that would force him to look at her work. "Mac and

I took the toy from his idea through the design stages. We made a lot of drawings and color renderings.''

"They're wonderful," Tia told her.

"Thank you." Suzanne pointed to the end counter at three model Holly Bearys with cutaway sides. "After a while we moved on to making models until we hit on something we both thought perfect."

Mac said nothing, just nodded and glanced back at Suzanne with the same bland expression. It was obvious he was angering Suzanne, and yet, he held his silence like a shield. The reason weakened Tia's knees. This office was a testament to how closely Mac and Suzanne had worked on this project. He had to be terrified he'd give himself away.

Tia forced a bright smile. "I can't believe the amount of work that's gone into making this teddy bear."

"Exactly," Suzanne said as though that was the point and should be appreciated. She smoothed the hair at her nape. "Anyway, once we knew what we wanted, I went looking for the right fabric. I had to have something soft and plush, yet fireproof. I think we came up with a great one."

Tia fingered the various fabrics on the workboard, trying to act interested. But her hand wasn't as steady as she'd like and she dropped it immediately. Praying Suzanne hadn't noticed. Wouldn't wonder about it later.

"What about the blueprint for Holly Beary?" Mac broke his silence.

Both women lurched slightly.

"I assume it's in Mac's safe." Suzanne shrugged. "That was where he was keeping it."

"I guess I'll just make sure of that," he said.

"Come on, Tia. Ms. Chang, I assume you've got everything running smoothly?"

"Yes." She spit the word as though he'd insulted her. She followed them back to the shipping-dock area and made straight for the new arrivals, which she began inspecting again.

The cold air wrapped itself around Tia with fresh vigor. She moved to where Suzanne worked, lifted one of the bears from the carton and did her own analysis, checking the seams and the details of construction as she hadn't before.

Suzanne gawked at her, alert. Edgy. Why? The quality of the bear *was* exceptional. Bad vibes coursed the short distance separating her from Suzanne. An unpleasant notion took hold of Tia. "Where are the bears made? In Asia?"

Suzanne blinked and swallowed quickly. "Why, no. In Mexico."

Tia didn't know this woman, but she could swear she was lying. And she could think of only one reason for such a lie. Something dark and ugly slithered through her mind, tripped her pulse. "It's a fine product."

"I'm particularly pleased with it."

"You should be," Mac told her, reaching for Tia's elbow and applying a gentle force that said it was time to move on.

She resisted his silent urging to leave. "Have you been to the factory yourself, Ms. Chang?"

Sweat dampened Tia's underarms. The last thing Mac needed on top of a spy in his company were charges of hiring a sweatshop to make his toys. That kind of negative publicity could wipe a product out.

"Yes, I have visited the factory." Suzanne's tiny

chin shot up and defiance flared her nostrils. "Several times."

Tia felt the pressure on her elbow tense, and knew Suzanne lied. Her stomach felt like a pin cushion. They needed to check the cost sheets. Maybe even investigate the factory personally. She quit resisting Mac's attempt to move her away from Suzanne.

Once they were out of anyone's earshot, Mac said, "I only recall her taking one visit to the factory. Why did she lie?"

Tia shook her head. "We're going to have to find out."

"Come on, then. I want to talk to Fred Vogler next."

"Okay—in a minute, though." She felt sick with worry...and fear. She needed some cold water on her face. "I have to hit the ladies' room after all the coffee I've consumed. Be right back."

Feeling as though the devil himself stalked her, Tia fled in the direction she'd seen Stewy going earlier. The rest rooms were in a dark corner of the warehouse behind several stacks of cartons. She slipped into the narrow pathway. The hair on her nape prickled. She moved more quickly. Bumped boxes. Made herself slow down. She wouldn't get back to Mac at all if she hyperventilated and passed out.

A hand landed on her shoulder. Her heart stopped for two full beats. She was spun around.

"Buddy. Damn you." She glared at him.

"Hey, T. A little jumpy, huh?"

She drew a ragged breath. "I'm understandably edgy. Too much coffee and too little sleep. After all, my fiancé lost his brother yesterday."

Bud Gibson winced as though she'd struck him.

"Mac Coy was one good guy."

Tia hugged herself. "Did he know what a 'good guy' you are?"

Bud's eyes darkened. Fear slithered through Tia. It was one thing to have pushed his buttons when he was a scrawny kid, but he had grown into a man who could overpower her within seconds if he chose. Why hadn't she kept her mouth shut?

He grasped her by both upper arms.

Tia yelped.

He leaned close. His breath smelled of onions. "No one here knows about my record. And I want it to stay that way. You understand?"

Tia recalled the gun he'd had earlier. How had a convicted felon gotten hold of a gun? Would he use it to make sure she kept silent about him? "You're hurting me, Buddy. Let go."

"Not until you promise to keep your mouth shut about me, T."

"I promise."

"Good." He released her and stepped back. "You don't tell Mr. Coy about me and I won't tell him about you."

Chapter Six

Mac stood stock-still, listening to the bustle of work going on all around him, drawing solace in its reassurance that life continued despite the worst of blows. Despite death. But for all the activity, all the people within shouting distance, he felt utterly alone.

Stripped of his own identity, he had nothing in common with his employees. Knew nothing personal about any of them. Not that this was a bad thing at the moment. The less dialogue between himself and them, the better. He couldn't afford to slip and say something wrong. Something to give himself away.

But it was damned difficult to keep remembering what he wasn't supposed to know. To keep his mouth shut in the face of a blatant lie—like Suzanne's. He'd really wanted to protest when she said she'd visited the factory in Mexico several times. There was only the one time he knew of. Why had she exaggerated? And why had Tia looked worried when she'd asked the question?

A chill swept over him, through him. He shifted around, half expecting to find Grant's killer standing behind him or watching him intently from close quarters. But no one was nearby. In fact, as far as he could tell, the only person looking at him was Tia. She hurried toward him, frowning, her face ashen. Alarm shot through him. What was wrong? Then he realized she was frowning at *him.*

He tensed, and as he did, he realized he'd slipped into his usual slouch. Damn. He had to stay alert. Watch his posture. His stance. His mannerisms. Doing the walk he'd practiced throughout the night, he started toward Tia…and stepped right out of one of the oversize loafers. He stubbed his toe on the hard concrete, stumbled, lurched forward, arms flailing. Cursing, he caught himself before he landed on the floor like a clumsy oaf, but not before his ears burned.

"Are you all right?" Tia looked frightened—as though she thought he'd been shot. Her concern stoked the burning in his ears and warmed his heart.

"Stepped right out of the damned shoe," he grumbled, retrieving the offending loafer and slipping it on again.

"Oh." She bit the sides of her cheek to keep from laughing with relief.

Heat climbed his neck. "This suit is uncomfortable enough, but these shoes… I have to keep my toes curled to keep them on."

"We should have put tissue in them."

"Tomorrow." He touched her elbow, enjoying the sensation of holding her delicate arm so possessively, wondering what it would be like to possess this woman, to be possessed by her. The idea enfolded him, started a fierce smoldering in his belly. But self-loathing chased the fire from him. She'd been his brother's fiancée. He had no right to her. Not now. Not ever. "Come on, let's talk to Fred."

Mac forced his mind to the possible guilt of his

operations manager. He'd known Fred for five years. Considered him a loyal and responsible employee, a trusted friend. But then, he'd thought that of all his managers. And one of them was a traitor and a murderer.

But how easy would it have been for Fred to lay his hands on the blueprints? Or on one of the precious prototypes?

Fred Vogler sat with his back to them, his rotund body perched on the center of a stool, a phone to his ear. Mac cleared his throat. Fred tensed, then spun around. A wooden matchstick hung from the corner of his mouth, and his bullfrog eyes, the watery green of a lily pad, swept Tia and "Grant." He cut off his conversation so abruptly it seemed it might have been personal.

But he said, "Just a client who needed reassurance about the delivery of the bears."

Mac stiffened. Another lie from one of his trusted. Fred's job entailed arranging for warehousing of merchandise before it went out and for the shipping, who took what to where. He never talked to customers. Not unless a shipment needed tracing—then he'd turn the actual tracing over to Stewy. Who had he really been talking to? Mac supposed he'd have to check the company phone records.

Meanwhile, maybe he could figure something out now. He glanced at the notepad near Fred's elbow. Someone had drawn what looked like teddy bears all over it. "What's that?"

Fred followed Mac's gaze, his froggy eyes opening a tad wider. He snatched the sheet of paper from the pad and stuffed it into his pocket. He gnawed the matchstick. "Nothing. Just some doodling of Stewy's.

He thinks he's going to be the next Gary Larsen—you know, the guy who draws those funny animal cartoons?''

"Nothing wrong with ambition," Mac said. "As long as he's not seeking this new career on my time." *Or ripping me off.*

"Don't worry, Mr. Coy. I keep Stewy hopping." Fred smiled at Tia, making no attempt to hide his blatant admiration. But it was the hint of lust in the bulgy eyes that got to Mac. He inched toward Tia, that sense of possessiveness rearing inside him anew. Or was he actually worried she needed protection from this man because he was a killer?

Mac couldn't be sure. After all, if the doodling on the paper was Stewy's, why had Fred stuffed it into his pocket? Fred was a frustrated artist. His paintings had never taken off. Was he trying something new? A series on teddy bears—much as Red Skelton had painted clowns—hoping to capitalize on Holly Beary's success? "What's the shipping schedule looking like?"

Fred shifted the matchstick to the other side of his mouth and studied Mac a beat too long. Mac's pulse wobbled. Had his question been a bit too knowledge-able? No. Sooner or later anyone would have thought to ask the man responsible for getting merchandise shipped to the consumer whether or not the new schedule could be met.

Fred consulted a clipboard beside the phone. "I've been getting the expected grumbling about the closed window time. Three weeks before Christmas every-body's scheduled to the max. But my ducks are lining up. We'll get it done."

TIA AND MAC slipped into the elevator, grateful for the immediate warmth it offered and the privacy. Mac's brow was knit, the gleam in his eyes distant. She touched his arm. "What do you think?"

He made a face. "I think both Fred and Suzanne are jittery. Both lied. Nothing major. Nothing worth the hassle of lying."

"So why do it?" she asked, understanding his wonder.

He told her what they'd lied about. Tia frowned. "You're right. Both of those things are easily checked out. We'd only have to call the factory in Mexico. Only look at the phone records here to see who Fred called. Yet both took the chance 'Grant' wouldn't know they were lying."

"But why lie at all?" He shook his head. "Fred could have said he was speaking to a freight company. Suzanne had no need to say anythi—"

He broke off, his gaze pinning Tia as though he'd just remembered something. "Suzanne didn't lie until you pushed her about the factory in Mexico. Why? And why did you look so concerned about how often she'd visited?"

Tia felt the heat drain from her face. She hadn't wanted to tell him her concerns about sweatshops until she could brace him first. But before she could form an answer, the elevator doors swung open at the second floor. A woman stood there, looking frazzled.

"B—er, Ms. Novak?" Concern etched Mac's face as he stepped from the elevator.

"Bijou, please. I can't stand the formality. It goes against everything Mac stood for." She didn't even blink, apparently not registering the fact that 'Grant' could only be more formal if he wore a tuxedo.

Bijou carried a good twenty-five pounds of excess weight. Her frosted hair was twisted into a French roll with pencils poking out at both sides of her head like a pair of chopsticks. Dark circles underscored her aqua eyes. She twisted her hands together. Stressed? Or distressed? Tia eyed her curiously, trying to figure out which.

''Mac's'' death had hit several of his employees hard. But a murderer might be feeling stress, too. The stress of getting away with it. Was this woman a loyal company representative...or a cold-blooded killer?

Apparently misreading Tia's look of curiosity, Bijou blurted, ''I'm head of sales. I work with the retail buyers. Toys R 4 Kids, Discount-Mart, Jmart, Bullseye, Cee-Say Toys. Those are the biggest toy retailers.''

Tia nodded but said nothing, waiting for Mac's lead. He seemed not to know what to say, or else he feared he'd say too much. He straightened his cuffs, tugged at his tie. She would have smiled if she didn't know how uncomfortable he felt.

Their silence had Bijou fidgeting, twisting her hands together more agitatedly. ''We've shown the toy four or more times this past year to the buyers from each chain—at the varying stages of its development. They were all highly impressed with the finished product last February.''

''February?'' Tia asked, pulling her gaze from Mac's arresting face, something she found harder to do as the day progressed.

''Yeah, the annual Toy Fair in New York City,'' Bijou explained in an incredulous voice, as though anyone who hadn't heard of the Toy Fair was an alien from outer space. "Don't you people know any-thing?"

"Not much," Mac said. "We're talking to each department head and learning as quickly as we can."

Bijou bit her lower lip like a petulant child, as though she feared this whole mess would just get worse with these two amateurs at the helm. "I suppose you were coming to see me next?"

They hadn't been, but Mac lied, "Yes."

Guilt flashed in Bijou's aqua eyes. She pushed up a stray strand of hair at the nape of her neck, managing to look like a person in dire need of a cigarette. "I just stepped out into the hall for a minute. I had to get away from the damned phones. They've been ringing off the hook."

Mac frowned. "I told Ms. Rice to take care of that."

"If the only people calling were concerned customers, then maybe one person could handle it. But everyone's been calling to express their condolences, from the mayor of Renton to the governor of the state. Mac would have been touched to know how many people cared about him.

"Can't imagine anyone would miss me." She sniffed and turned aside, then quickly back toward them. Her eyes were dry. "Anyhow, I told Nancy to put the customers through to me. Don't want them canceling orders and going with that ripoff firm in Asia. I've been calling my own list and taking the calls from those buyers who get to me first. Not everyone has heard. But the toy world is a small community in many ways. News will travel fast. Mac was well respected in this industry."

Tia saw "Grant's" ears redden and knew he was

embarrassed by the praise. Maybe even surprised. However, how much *he* was liked in this industry was the least of his concerns. Always the toys and the children came first. Her heart warmed, speeding delicious tendrils of longing through her. She resisted the ache, the urge to move closer to him, holding her muscles rigid. She feared her growing attraction to him almost as much as she feared the killer finding out Mac was still alive.

Bijou ran her gaze over Mac.

Mac squirmed beneath her perusal. Bijou was that rare breed who could size a person up while talking rapid-fire, a talent few developed and fewer honed. She was a great salesperson.

She took a deep breath and wrung her hands some more. "Is there anything else I can tell you?"

"I can't think of anything." Mac gave her his best Grant stare, narrowing his eyes as he'd seen his twin do when recanting a tale of questioning suspects. "But if I do, you'll be available?"

"Of course." A grin pulled the corner of her mouth, and he realized he'd sounded like some TV cop. His ears warmed. He started to reach for his glasses, but caught himself in time. He was an idiot in an Armani suit. God, how had Grant carried this off? His shortcomings threatened to unnerve him. He struggled to maintain his posture. Grasping his anger helped.

Bijou poked at one of the pencils in her hair. "At least assure me the bears will go out on time."

Mac gave her Grant's finger-thumb gun gesture, feeling more like a failure than ever. "According to Fred Vogler, there's no problem."

She rolled her eyes. "Fred? Hah! I'll trust something he says when pigs fly."

Mac's stomach fell. "You think Fred lied to me?"

Bijou's brows shot up. She waved her hand dismissively. "Oh, don't listen to me. I'm in a foul mood. It's been that kind of morning. Guess I should get back to my desk."

"Why don't you take a few minutes in the lunchroom?" Mac suggested. He'd swear she was more high-strung than usual. He could understand the stress, but what was with the doom-and-gloom attitude? It was almost as though she expected disaster at any moment. Did she know something he should be told? Anxiety struck his heart. Would she tell him if he asked? Or would she lie to him, too? Was every one of his handpicked employees someone other than the person he thought him or her to be?

Bijou looked taken back at his suggestion, as though she hadn't heard him correctly.

"Really," he said. "Your phone ear probably needs a rest. Have something to eat. Freshen your coffee."

Bijou studied him intently. "For a minute there— you sounded just like Mac."

Mac blanched.

"Oh, there I go again upsetting the applecart. You're probably nothing like Mac at all. Are you?"

Tia and Mac stepped back into the elevator. Bijou stood where she was, studying Mac with those shrewd aqua eyes until the doors closed.

"God, Mac, does she suspect?"

"I don't know." His jacket felt damp everywhere it touched his skin. "I could use some lunch myself.

Why don't we get away from here for a while—run out to Issaquah and eat at Gilman Village?''

"Wouldn't you rather go somewhere you can kick off those shoes for a while? Take off that tie?"

He sighed. "That sounds like heaven, but where?"

"I know just the place. My place. We can call from the car phone and have a pizza delivered. I need to pick up some clothes and check my mail and phone messages."

TIA'S APARTMENT COMPLEX overlooked the expanded shopping area near Gilman Village. She let them through the security gate and then to a three-story building near the end. "I'm on the top floor."

"Do you live alone?" Mac asked as he pulled the Porsche into a spot near the switchback stairs.

"Yes." Tia had discovered the undesirability of having a roommate during her two years at Crimble Industries. She'd moved out and moved on. Moved into this secured complex. It gave her a moderate sense of protection. Nevertheless, she kept her personal items to a minimum—just in case someone slipped past the safeguards and into her well-ordered life.

One such invasion would last her a lifetime.

"No pets, either?" He asked as they reached the third-floor landing.

"With my schedule I'd have to constantly farm out pet chores to others, and that doesn't seem fair to them or to a pet."

"Good point. I'd have a dog, but when I'm working on a toy, I sometimes forget to eat. Couldn't do that to an animal."

Tia laughed, the sweet tinkling sound floating on

the crisp air and wending straight to his ravaged heart. She grinned up at him. "More likely the dog would remind you to feed him and then you'd remember to eat too."

He smiled wryly. "I hadn't thought of that."

She unlocked the door. "Here it is. Home sweet home."

The apartment was neat and small, like Tia. But there the similarity ended. The decor had the feel of something selected from a catalog, every piece a perfect blend of tone and hue, every item complementary. All the washed blues and pale peaches and timid creams blended into something inoffensive and pleasant, but somehow plastic.

It startled Mac. He'd have thought she'd go for bolder colors—something deep and green like her mesmerizing eyes. And why were there no photographs or knickknacks or magazines adorning the tables? Not even a plant, silk or real. He supposed plants might fall into the "pet care" category, but a cactus would have thrived in the room.

"Make yourself at home," Tia said, shrugging out of her coat. "The pizza should be here any minute."

She headed into the short hallway. To her bedroom, he supposed. He wanted to follow, to see if that room was where he'd find the real Tia. But along with the temptation came a slamming jolt of desire. He kicked off Grant's shoes, loosened the tie and slipped off the jacket. His shirt felt as though someone had damp-pressed it to him. He undid the top button and tugged the shirt from his skin, then dropped onto the sofa. He'd really like to take off the shirt and let it dry out, but the thought of being half-naked in Tia's apartment weakened the reins he'd tightened on his hunger for her. As blood began pooling hot and hard in his groin again, he groaned softly. Man, he couldn't recall a more uncomfortable morning in his life.

TIA GAZED UNCOMFORTABLY around her bedroom. It was as sparsely decorated as the living room. Only the essential bed and dresser. The closet had mirrored doors and there was access into the lone bathroom. She'd stayed with the same color scheme here as in the living room. Nice and bland. Nothing jarring. Nothing personal. She liked it that way.

No reminders of her past. Grant had once said all she needed was a Bible in the top drawer of the nightstand to finish the feeling that you were in a motel room in Anywhere, USA. He hadn't understood. Even after she'd explained it to him.

She glanced at her answering machine. Five calls. The knot in her stomach wound tighter. She could count on one hand those who knew her phone number. And today there was one less. Steeling herself, she sank onto the bed and pushed the button.

A woman's voice sliced the weighted silence. "Tia, dear, it's Molly. Are you coming for Christmas Day? Please let me know."

Tia stopped the recorder. Molly Bowen, her foster mother. The invitation hardly inspired Tia's holiday spirit. Oh, Molly meant well, but while the woman who'd raised her had been kind and gentle, she'd been emotionally distant. Cool. Not exactly a nurturing soul. Tia realized now Molly wouldn't allow herself to get close or attached to any of her foster kids because they didn't stay around long. She was always afraid of loving, then losing them. And she had. All but Tia—the child no one wanted.

Tia hugged herself against the old pain and pushed the recorder again. "Hi, babe. I know you're out of town, but in case you called your machine, well, er, ah, I think we need to have a long talk when you get back."

Grant. Her heart twisted with pain and that damnable guilt.

She fast-forwarded the tape to the next message. "Hi, babe. Me again. Thought I should tell you that I'm investigating something for Mac. He's staying at my place and I'm pretending to be him. It's kind of hairy. Some of his people have been giving me the old evil eye as though they suspect I'm not Mac. I haven't had this much fun since junior high."

Her body felt like a lump of cold rock. The fourth message began. "Hi, babe. The investigation has me running in circles. I don't want Mac to know, but if I don't vent to someone, I'll break down and tell him. I've started a background check on his department heads. Seems he handpicked these people on their say-so and his own gut instinct. He'd be surprised and appalled at some of the information my operatives have unearthed about these 'trustworthy' employees. The data is compiled in my office computer. No sense upsetting Mac with details he never wanted, unless it becomes necessary. See you soon."

Tia's limbs had gone leaden. She stared dumbfounded at the machine for a whole ten seconds, then rewound the fourth message and listened to it again. "Mac, come in here."

He appeared in the doorway, shirttails hanging out of his slacks, a slice of pizza in one hand, the very picture of a man unwinding after a tough time of it.

When had the pizza arrived? She hadn't heard the doorbell ring.

Mac glanced around the room and surprise registered on his face. Then his gaze fell on her and he seemed to flinch, all at once losing the casual air. If anything he seemed ill at ease. Worse than he'd been at the plant.

"You have to hear this." Tia patted the bed beside her. Mac just stared at the spot for several seconds before moving hesitantly toward her. He sat down on the very edge of the mattress, perching as though he might leap up at any moment. She covered his hand with her own, anchoring him. She felt him tense and squeezed harder. "It's Grant."

Mac looked down at her, shock swirling beneath his querulous, unspoken glance. The slice of pizza dangled from his hand, forgotten. She wanted to spare him Grant's comments on his employees, on his selection of them. But she could think of no way to do that. Her chest hurt. She rewound the tape and played the message again.

Her eyes locked with Mac's and she felt as if the room receded, leaving only the two of them in this time, this space, linked by their grief. Her hand tightened on his; the warmth was the one real thing in this illusory moment.

Mac seemed to listen intently. His eyes narrowed, the lids shutting completely as though he'd suffered a physical blow when Grant claimed he'd be surprised and appalled to learn the truth about his employees. That had to cut to the very quick, slice through his self-image. Her heart ached for Mac. She wanted to do more than hold his hand. She wanted to hold him, comfort him. Love him. Prove to him he was wiser than his brother proclaimed.

Tia stopped the tape at the end of the message.

The pain on Mac's face tore at her soul. She yearned to touch his cheek, absorb his distress, carry it away. But she feared he'd misinterpret it as pity and so did nothing, except struggle to keep the pressure of her hand steady.

"Play it again." The words choked from Mac. He listened this time with his eyes open. Not one flinch. Steely determination and acceptance controlled his expression. When the tape ended, he let out a huge breath. He rolled to his feet, a man in need of expelling excess frustration. Unspoken devils. "I hadn't thought to look for information at Quell, and Grant's secretary didn't mention anything about the case when I called this morning. She was too busy offering me condolences."

"We'll have to go there. Get into his computer."

"Yes."

"But there's one more message." She frowned at him and rose from the bed. "Maybe that's from Grant, too."

Mac tensed as though braced for another mental jolt.

With a trembling hand she reached for the button and played the last message. "Hi, Tia. Just calling to see how you are. How Grant is doing. Call me when you get time. I really need to talk to you about something."

Tia gave Mac a relieved glance. "That was my friend, Ginny. Bud Gibson's sister. She was with me when we heard about 'your' death. I'll call her later."

Tia wanted to call her now. To find out why she

hadn't told her about Buddy's working for Mac. Was that what Ginny wanted to discuss, too? "I'm sure you want to go directly to Quell."

"No. As much as I'd like that information before returning to the plant, we'll have to go to Quell after hours. It was bad enough passing as him over the phone. I don't dare risk a face-to-face encounter with Grant's associates—not while I'm impersonating Grant."

She nodded. "I understand. You've got enough on your hands with your own people."

"My own people..." A bitter laugh spilled from him. He glanced at the limp slice of pizza as though it was a dead rat. "Where's your garbage?"

THE FIRST PLACE they headed when they returned to the plant was Mac's office. A pile of telephone-message slips occupied a large section on his desk. Awed, he scanned the messages. "I had no idea so many people cared whether I lived or—"

Nancy Rice poked her head through the doorway. Mac bit off his statement, his heart leaping. He'd forgotten himself and spoken as though he was Mac, not Grant. He felt his shirt getting damp again. He had to be more careful. Dear God, had she heard? He studied her pretty face, her wide brown eyes, but saw nothing more worrisome than concern for him.

She ignored Tia completely and started toward him, batting her eyelashes at him of all things. "I hope I'm not interrupting."

"No," he said hoarsely in response to his blunder. But he could see she thought he was reacting to her. He lowered his voice. "What do you need?"

"I wasn't sure what to do with those." She gave

a shake of her blond head and pointed to the messages. "Mostly they're inquiries about the funeral. Is a date set yet?"

Mac's gut tensed. "No.

He wasn't sure when the police would release the body, but he didn't want to say that.

"What should I tell people when they ask?" Nancy frowned, looking like a fluttery airhead incapable of making a decision on her own. What kind of game was she playing and why? Ice layered his gut at the possibilities. Nancy managed this office like a boat captain running an ocean liner. So why was she acting like a naive ingenue? A flirt? Coming on to Grant— with no respect for his being engaged?

She repeated, "What should I tell people when they ask?"

Mac ran his hand across his hair. "Say the arrangements are being made and we'll run an announcement in the paper as soon as everything is settled."

"Okay." As Nancy walked out the door, he met Tia's gaze. She gave him a sympathetic smile. He shook his head, then turned back to all the messages, touching the stack absently. He felt like George Bailey in *It's a Wonderful Life* discovering he had a wealth of friends. That his life had touched others in ways he'd never expected made a difference. There were names of people he hadn't spoken to in years. Mac's heart swelled with such emotion he couldn't deal with it. Couldn't deal with these messages, either.

He pulled open the top drawer of his desk and swept them inside. As he did, a strip of red foil peeked from beneath the messages. His gaze narrowed. Amid the messages there was a small gift-wrapped box. Mac froze. The attached tag read, "To Grant, from Santa." His pulse kicked. He shouted, "Nancy!"

"What is it?" Tia rushed to his side and fell silent as she spotted the gift.

Nancy reappeared in the doorway. "Is something wrong?"

Mac knew he'd better not make too much of this. Not raise her suspicions. Somehow he managed to keep his voice calm, his hand from trembling as he held the small package up for her to see. "Did you notice who left this on my desk?"

She came unnecessarily close to him and studied the box, then shrugged, shaking her head. "It wasn't there when I left the messages."

His control of his patience faltered. "Who was in this office while we were gone?"

She shrugged again. "Gee, I've been so busy with the phones, I couldn't say I noticed anyone."

"Oh, Grant." Tia sidled up to Mac and snaked her arm through his as though warning Nancy off her territory. "Now you've gone and spoiled my surprise."

Mac blushed, and Nancy seethed prettily, glaring at Tia. "Guess that solves the mystery, boss." She left in a snit.

Laughing softly, Mac shut the door behind her. "Quick thinking, Ms. Larken. Thank you."

Tia's eyes were as round as tree ornaments. "Just open it."

Mac ripped off the wrapping. Another Lei Industries box. He set it on the table between them, lifted the lid slowly. Inside were a matchstick—the type

Fred favored—a mitten like Holly Beary's and a folded piece of paper.

"It's a typewritten note." He held the paper in a hand trembling with rage. "It says, *Hold the lighted match to the mitten.* Mac did as instructed. To his horror the mitten began burning. He dropped it into the water pitcher on the table and swore. "It's not flame-retardant. If this gets into the hands of even one child…"

"Can't we warn stores about this? Call some media-news magazines?"

"And offer what proof? We don't have Lei's product here. All we have is a piece of charred fabric that could have come from anywhere." Mac felt sick.

Chapter Seven

"Mac, we'll get the real Holly Beary released before that piece of junk imitation can leave Lei's warehouse." Tia spoke softly but with fierce determination. Her emerald eyes, alight with confidence, as brilliant as Christmas stars against a winter sky, made him almost believe.

But she knew the odds were stacked against them, knew they weren't just fighting the enemy in Taiwan, but the enemy within. He rubbed his jaw in frustration and recalled again Tia's concern about the factory in Mexico. His tie felt like a garrote. "What were you going to tell me in the elevator before Bijou interrupted us?"

Tia blew out a wobbly breath and squared her shoulders as though he'd turned the tables and poked her in the back. Her hands began moving, gesturing for him to stay calm. Like being told not to get upset, it heightened his anxiety.

"Really, it's probably nothing," she said. "I just wondered whether or not Suzanne had inspected the factory to be certain it wasn't a sweatshop. Look at what happened to Kathie Lee Gifford and her clothing line. Innocent people are often duped by factory owners. Call me overly careful. Or a worrier. I just think it's better to err on the side of caution than to find out in the morning news that Coy Toys' top seller is manufactured by ten-year-olds in some Mexican village."

Mac's office door opened.

He didn't notice. He stared at Tia. Disbelief shredded what remained of his composure. His shirt clung to his body like a wetsuit without talcum powder. "A sweatshop?"

"Oh, how aptly put. My opinion exactly." A skinny man with hair the artificial gold of a sequined gown waltzed into the room, interrupting the conversation as though this was not his boss's office, not the boss and his fiancée he was barging in on. "This is the most demanding job I've ever had. I'm so glad you concur. Your brother never would admit it. But then, you probably knew what a workaholic that man was. Morning, noon and nighttime, too. Like he hadn't heard of the nine-to-five workday."

Tia and Mac gaped at the intruder. He seemed to finally notice.

"Oh, how rude of me. I don't suppose either of you remember me from this morning's meeting." He stretched his hand toward Mac. "Will Holden. Head of publicity."

Mac ignored the proffered hand. "Yes. I think Ms. Larken and I both remember you, Mr. Holden."

"Oh, please, couldn't we make it Will and Grant? My salary doesn't deserve the prestige of formalities."

Mac eyed Will with barely concealed disdain. He was used to Will's "too much work for too little pay" diatribe. Not a month went by that he didn't ask for an increase in his take-home.

"I do have a rather…er, delicate request, Grant. I mean, now that the launch has been moved up and I'll be doing twice as much as normal, well, I was wondering about a raise."

Mac pressed his lips together, stifling a moan. Could this man have chosen a more inappropriate time? What was his problem? He earned a fair wage for the work he did. Better than fair. Until now Mac hadn't thought to wonder why it wasn't enough. But now suspicions flew through his head like a flurry of snowflakes. "I don't think you've been asked to do anymore than anyone else. Why should you deserve special compensation?"

"Well, Grant, the thing is…" Will moved closer as though he were about to reveal a secret. "Mac, he, ah…promised it to me…before…you know…"

Like hell I did! Anger gathered in Mac, a churning, boiling rage, a volcano ready to spew lava on this unsuspecting man. Dammit. Another bald-faced liar. It was a bloody epidemic. He wanted to grab Will by his scrawny neck and toss him out of the office.

"See, the thing is," Will continued, oblivious to how close he stood to a mass of roiling fury, "Mac said if the toy is as big a hit as he expected it to be, the raise would be forthcoming."

Mac curled his hands into fists. He'd said no such thing. It was, however, an unspoken promise. Whatever success the toy generated would be shared by all those who'd made it possible. Why, then, was Will seeking his money before the launch? An ugly thought punched his gut. Did Will know "Grant" would fail? "Why don't you show us what you've arranged for publicity?"

"Well, sure, but I'd rather you waited until tomorrow, Grant. I mean, this morning wasn't much notice and I'm not ready yet." He waved his hands like twin fans. "Tomorrow, okay? Now...about my money?"

"There won't be any bonuses until Holly Beary begins generating some income." Mac choked down his anger. Reaching for his missing glasses, he caught himself, quickly running his forefinger down his nose as though that was what he'd meant to do. Sweat beaded his upper lip. "All extra funds are being funneled into the launch."

Will sighed and plopped his hand on his hip. "Oh, well, you can't blame a guy for trying." He headed to the door, turning back at the last second. "Tomorrow I'll have masterpieces for your viewing."

Mac faced Tia. "What did you make of that?"

She looked as though she didn't know whether to laugh or proclaim Will Holden the killer. "Nervy. Is he always that...brazenly rude?"

"I never paid it much mind. But, yes, I suppose he is."

"He seems to have an overblown ego."

"That's putting in mildly." Mac grinned wryly. "Will's a good artist, and he has the necessary media connections, but he's always hitting me up for more money. I never thought to wonder why until now."

She frowned at him. "Would he sabotage the company if someone offered him the right monetary incentive?"

"Seems a good possibility. Maybe there's something in his private life making him desperate for cash." Maybe Grant had found out what the something was. Mac itched to get a look at Grant's computer. But that had to wait until tonight. "I'll tell you one thing—he's now the fourth liar out of my trusted five."

He explained the lie to her.

"Six." Tia brushed her hair behind one ear, a gesture he found distracting, especially when she tipped her head to one side as she was doing now. "You forgot Nancy."

He tried not to notice how shiny Tia's hair was in the glinting lights of the Christmas decorations. Tried ignoring the musical lilt in her voice that stirred his blood with improper images. "Yes, well, so far Nancy hasn't lied. She's just acting completely out of character."

"Is she?" Tia gave him a pointed gaze. "Or is this just the first time you've seen her around a man who turns her on?"

The tips of Mac's ears warmed, but he didn't know whether to be complimented or insulted. Nancy had never given him a second glance...until he looked like Grant. His gaze locked with Tia's. He knew he shouldn't stare, but for the life of him, he couldn't look away. Something about her reached out to him, into him. A silent yearning that grabbed his soul, that spoke to a deep thirst he'd never been able to quench. Did she know that feeling, too? Was that why he wanted to pull her into his arms and never let go?

"I wish we could get the information from Grant's computer now," she said.

"Me, too. But since we can't, why don't we pay the electronics department a visit? See if Gwen Gallagher will make the liars number five?"

"Whatever you say," she teased. "You're the boss."

"Oh, wait." He snapped his fingers. "I want to check on the blueprints while I'm thinking about them."

He led her over to a door at the back of the room. It was a compact walk-in closet, full of office supplies. He knelt, moved a box of paper from a corner wall, then lifted a patch of rug that was attached to a thick slab of wood. Concealed in the floor was a small safe. Mac quickly did the combination. Tension banded his chest. He pulled the door toward him and peered into the dark well. "As far as I can tell, everything is as I left it a week ago."

She dropped to her knees beside him, her alluring scent stealing into his nostrils, whetting his senses. Their shoulders bumped. Mac reached out to steady her. Her nose was inches from his, her mouth a whisper away. Her green eyes glistened, warm and welcoming, full of longing. Every other thought but Tia fled his mind.

As though it were the most natural thing in the world, he pulled her to him. He grazed her lips with his, hesitantly, a child tasting a first piece of candy, testing the sweetness, finding he quite liked it and committing himself for another, larger portion of the heady delicacy.

Totally mystifying him, Tia responded to his kiss like a woman surrendering to the man of her dreams. Her reaction fed his confidence, inflamed his affection. She welcomed his invasion of her mouth, lifted her hands to his face, to his hair, pressed her body to his. His blood burned hot through his veins, tightened in his groin with need so fierce it was honeyed agony.

A tiny voice in the back of his brain warned him to break away before he went too far, before he embarrassed them both. The hum of passion in his ears robbed him of his will, drowning out the tiny voice. He cupped her bottom in both hands, drawing her to his desire. She moaned his name softly against his lips.

"Guess my timing is a little off," Nancy Rice said.

Mac and Tia jerked apart. Tia scooted to her feet, straightening her sweater, her face flushed pink. Mac couldn't recover as quickly. He stayed on his knees and looked up at Nancy over his shoulder.

"You might try knocking next time." His voice rasped with annoyance and unspent ardor. But he felt like a child caught opening presents before Christmas. "What do you want?"

Nancy fell silent. She was studying him, her clever mind racing so hard he could almost hear the cogs. Mac's heart plunged like a plane running on empty. Had he somehow given himself away? Had she heard Tia call him by name?

Nancy put her hand through her blond hair. "How did you know the combination to Mac's safe?"

Mac swallowed hard. "He gave it to me when he had the thing installed. I took the chance he hadn't changed—" Mac broke off. "Why am I explaining myself to you? I'm *your* boss."

"Well, of course." Nancy blushed, but she continued to study him for another beat or two—her Ms. Flirty side gone, the intelligent, suspicious Ms. Office Manager back in charge. "Is there something I can help you look for?"

He narrowed his eyes. "You have the combination to this safe?"

"Certainly. Mac gave it to me, too."

The tips of his ears burned. He'd forgotten. He had given it to Nancy once when he'd been out of town and needed some information he'd locked in here. "Thank you, but I can find what I'm after on my own. What did you want, Ms. Rice?"

"Oh." She smoothed her hands over her shapely body as if ironing out her composure. He braced for the certain personality switch. She didn't disappoint. She lifted her shoulder coquettishly. "I thought about who might have come in here while you and Ms. Larker were gone."

"Larken," Tia corrected.

"Yes, of course, dear." Nancy gave her a sugary smile.

"And?" Mac prodded, his patience with Nancy's game-playing stretched to the limit.

"And I think I saw Gwen heading this way around lunchtime."

Gwen? The information sat him back on his haunches. Why would the head of electronics be sending him pieces of an inferior Holly Beary? For that matter, where would she have gotten her hands on them? He could think of only one way she could have done that. It saddened him. He and Gwen Gallagher had all but started Coy Toys together. Of all his employees, he trusted her the most.

On the other hand, if she was the traitor, why send him these Santa gifts at all? It made no sense. He dismissed Nancy with a curt thank-you.

She beamed at him, then brushed past Tia as though she were garbage to be ignored. Tia waited five seconds, then peered around the closet door. "It's okay, Mac,'' she said, her voice neutral, with none of the husky warmth of a moment ago. "She's gone.''

So, Mac noted with utter disappointment, was the special closeness he and Tia had shared. She wouldn't look him in the eye. Although she was inches from him, she seemed a thousand miles away. She'd placed an invisible wall around herself, shutting him out, denying the attraction and response he'd drawn from her. Frustration rose within him. He didn't know much about male-female relationships. He was a great friend. Not a great lover.

How did he handle this? What did he say? That he was sorry he'd kissed her? Wanted her? No. Then he'd be a liar, too. For as guilty as he felt about betraying Grant, he couldn't dispute his longing for Tia. He might not know much about women, but he knew instinctively she'd be embarrassed if he mentioned their kiss. And he refused to cause her such distress.

"She gave me a scare for a second there.'' Tia pushed her hair behind her ear and tilted her head again. Her lips looked swollen and bruised. Thoroughly kissed. Needing more kisses. His desire simmered anew. He tamped it down.

Her lovely eyes narrowed. "Do you think she suspects anything?''

He guessed she was asking if Nancy had heard her cry out his name. He had no answer. Just a sinking suspicion. But he would spare Tia that concern. "Let's not drive ourselves crazy worrying about Nancy.''

"Okay.'' She looked unconvinced.

He reached into the safe and extracted a bound set of papers. The blueprints to Holly Beary. He stuffed them into his jacket pocket, relocked the safe, replaced the floor covering and stood. She was too close to him again. He ached to pull her back into his arms. Instead, he patted his chest where he'd placed the papers and felt his rapidly beating heart through the thick sheaf. "I'm going to put these in Grant's safe tonight. They'll be more secure there."

"Good plan." Her breath grazed his mouth.

Longing swept him. He needed out of these close quarters. "Let's go see what Gwen was doing here earlier."

"If she'll tell us the truth."

He laughed without mirth. "If she lies, then I guess I've got a full house."

THE ELECTRONICS LAB was on the second floor. Gwen Gallagher, Mac's company vice president, also served as head of this department. The entrance opened into an oblong office, with a laboratory against the back wall. The buzz of equipment flowed through the office like a radio tuned to Christmas carols: soft and apropos, but not distracting.

Gwen was seated at her desk before a computer, monitoring the crew working in the lab. She looked up as they came in and shut the door.

Gwen had the kind of beauty that wasn't discovered at first glance. Her features were classic, even unremarkable. But her skin was the creamy color of a Christmas moon, smooth and pale. She wore her shiny caramel brown, waist-length hair tied back with a leather thong. Keen blue eyes, the warm azure of a tropical sea, peered from beneath simple wire-rimmed glasses.

As that gaze landed on him, Mac had the sense that Gwen had been expecting him. She seemed to be offering him a silent welcome, as well as sympathy for their mutual loss of "Mac." It riveted Mac. Caught him off guard. But could he trust that her grief was genuine? Last week he would have believed it. But since hearing Grant's message to Tia, he felt like a fool for having taken these people at their word, for having trusted his instincts about them.

Gwen wiped a tear from her eye. "I'm sorry. I'm coping as best I can... Funny how little things can throw you off. I was just thinking about the first chip we produced for Holly Beary. We knew instinctively that we were close to getting what we wanted. So we pulled an all-night marathon. Around 2:00 a.m. we were so tired we started laughing about some silly thing and couldn't quit."

Mac remembered that late night, and his throat tightened at this hideous, necessary charade. If Gwen was innocent of this mess, she'd be humiliated when she found out he'd duped her.

"I wanted to see where Holly's heart was made." Tia stepped toward Gwen.

Gwen tore her gaze from Mac and eyed Tia coolly. She seemed displeased. At her request? Or at Tia herself? Mac frowned. Why would either upset Gwen?

She stood, removed her glasses and tucked them into the pocket of the lab coat she wore over precisely pressed forest green slacks. She pointed toward the back wall. "The actual chip is put together in the lab."

"Can we go in?" Tia asked.

"No." Gwen moved as if to block the entrance. "It's a sterile environment—like a medical lab, no dust or other contaminants. Only specified personnel are allowed in there."

"Such as the boss?" Mac appreciated her safety concerns. At least one of his employees seemed security conscious. But surely Gwen understood the new owners of Coy Toys would want to see their prize asset.

She gazed at him pointedly. "You haven't shown any interest before now."

This set Mac back on his heels. When had Grant last visited the lab? Had Gwen been here then? For the life of him, he couldn't recall. All he could think to say was, "I didn't own the company then."

Gwen blinked at him, looking as if he'd just crossed the boundaries of propriety. Twin dots colored her cheeks. "If you insist. You'll have to wear these sterile suits, caps, masks and surgical gloves. We can't have fibers or skin cells or hair or anything polluting the lab environment."

In his battle of wills with Gwen, Mac had forgotten the protective gear necessary to keep the lab sterile. There was no real reason for Tia and him to go into the lab. No reason to distract the crew. "You know, I think this could wait until next week—when things aren't so hectic."

The bright dots left Gwen's cheeks and her defensiveness slackened. She gave Mac a warm smile that sent a chill right to his toes. What the hell was he missing? Had this trusted assistant sold him out? Sold the very chip they'd worked to develop together? Hadn't she known she'd share in whatever profits the chip produced? Didn't that matter? "Nancy Rice said you'd stopped by my office around lunchtime. Was there something you wanted?"

She looked uncomfortable. "Well, yes. I'd like to speak to you alone, if Ms. Larken wouldn't mind."

Tia shrugged. "Of course not. I'll wait in the hall for you, Grant."

The moment the door closed behind Tia, Gwen launched herself at Mac, her arms snaked his waist, and her head pressed against his chest. "Oh, Grant. I'm so sorry about Mac. You must be devastated. I tried phoning you all last night, but there was no answer."

"I had the phone unplugged," he said dully, placing his arms around her from reflex. Patting her back in hopes of consoling her and getting her to regain her composure. He'd known this woman six years. She'd never shown a speck of emotion about anything that he could recall.

She lifted her head and Mac gazed down at her. "Why is Ms. Skycap here with you? You promised you'd tell her about us and get rid of her. I'm warning you, if you don't I will."

Mac gaped at Gwen. What the hell was she saying? She and Grant? When? How? Good God! Mac peeled her off him, holding her at arm's length by both upper arms. What was he supposed to do now? His mind raced like a pinwheel. She thought he was Grant. He had to act like Grant. But how was that? "I didn't see Tia until last night. She's been out of the country. I couldn't very well break up with her at the moment she came to console me about losing my brother."

"Why not?"

"Because I couldn't think about anything else but Mac."

She sighed and nodded. Understanding sympathy filled her eyes. "But you will do it soon? I'm tired of sneaking around. I want the world to know about us. And about the microchip *I* developed for Holly Beary. Right now I feel like I'm living one big lie."

"Lies," Mac murmured. "Yes, life does seem like that, doesn't it?"

"What?"

He shook himself. "Nothing."

"Promise me you'll tell that woman and soon. Because if you don't, Grant, I'll do it for you. I understood your not wanting Mac to know." She crossed her arms over her chest and seemed to lose her train of thought. "Though I think he was suspicious last week. He was acting really oddly toward me."

"How was that?"

"I couldn't put my finger on it quite." She scratched her head, thinking. "Did you notice the change in him?"

How did she know Grant and he had seen each other? "Ah, you mean that he'd shaved and cut his hair?"

"Well, yeah, that."

"He told me he did it in case people wanted to interview him after the toy was launched."

"That's what I mean. Does that even sound like Mac?"

Mac blanched. "I guess it was odd."

"Damn straight." She rocked her head from side to side. "I wrote it off at the time, figured it was my guilty conscience dogging me, but the more I think about it, the more I wonder."

Mac didn't like the new ninety-degree change this conversation was taking any better than the last one. "I can't keep Tia standing in the hall all afternoon. We'll talk later."

''It's not our talk you need to worry about, but your talk with her.''

Mac nodded and stumbled out into the hall. He stood there like a man in a fog. Brain-rattled. What was Grant into? Why would he cheat on Tia with Gwen? And what was *he* going to do about Gwen's ultimatum?

Chapter Eight

Rain pounded the top of the Porsche as Mac drove through early-evening traffic. The fierce meter matched the beat of the pain thrumming in his temples. His body ached with fatigue. Between the sleepless night, the ceaseless grief, the relentless guilt and the countless secrets, his head felt as though a herd of reindeer had stampeded across it.

Beside him Tia sat lost in her own thoughts. He supposed she was as exhausted as he, also dreading the long evening ahead. Even the prospect of finding some answers about his employees filled him with little enthusiasm after his visit to the lab.

His heart felt as heavy as the weather. How was he going to tell Tia about Grant and Gwen? He'd left the lab in a state of shock, brushing off her questions about why Gwen wanted to talk to him alone with a white lie. He feared she'd seen right through his tale. Had felt left out. Shut out. Better that, he figured, than his blurting what he'd just discovered. But he would have to tell her. And soon. Or Gwen would do it for him.

How would Tia react? How would she feel? He turned toward her, taking in her beloved profile. The notion of hurting her amplified his headache, added another stone to his heart. "Are you spending Christmas with your family?"

Tia's silence filled the inside of the car as though it were an entity of its own, as though he'd asked her a question as tough as the Daily Double on "Jeopardy." She turned to face him. In the rain-filtered headlights from the thick traffic he saw her expression was strained. "Didn't Grant tell you?"

Mac frowned, realizing Grant had shared little or nothing about Tia. He'd formed his own opinion of her by observation and conversation. He knew the kind of person she was, but nothing of her life or her family background. "Actually Grant and I didn't talk much about—"

"I don't have a family, Mac."

Surprise sawed his heart, spilling compassion through his veins. "I...I didn't know."

"I was raised in a foster home." Her voice sounded thick, faraway.

The noise of the heavy traffic faded in his desire to pull the car to the side of the road and gather her into his arms. He gripped the wheel more tightly and steered onto the freeway ramp. How had she ended up an orphan? He hesitated, then asked softly, "Did your parents die when you were young?"

Ten seconds passed before she said in a voice so tiny he strained to hear, "I was given up at birth for adoption."

A corner of Mac's heart seemed to tear off and lodge in his throat. He merged with the freeway traffic, accelerating to meet the higher speed. His heart raced like the powerful engine. Babies were a high commodity in the world of adoption. But she'd said she was raised in a foster home. That meant she hadn't been adopted. Why not?

"How come… Why didn't—" He broke off. He was overstepping his bounds. She had the right to tell him this if she wanted. But he had no right to pry.

"Why wasn't I adopted?" The strength had returned to her voice…along with something bitter. "Apparently I was a sickly baby. No one longs for a baby with medical problems."

He wanted to grasp her hand just as she'd clutched his in her apartment while they'd listened to Grant. Wanted to let her know he was there for her, as she'd been there for him. He lifted his hand from the gearshift, but Tia's hands were locked around her middle. His ears warming, he grasped the gearshift again. "So, you ended up in a foster home?"

"Yes."

He wanted to make sense of this, but he hadn't enough information. His cousin and her husband had adopted older children. Not every adoptive couple wanted babies. "Did your medical problems continue into childhood?"

"No." A quavery sigh issued from her. "I came close to being adopted…once…when I was eight."

"But?" He glanced at her.

She was hugging herself more tightly than before, as though against a deep-seated inner pain. "I stayed with this couple for a week. I thought it was a done deal. Then…they adopted someone else."

She sniffed and looked away from him. Mac eased the Porsche into the inside lane, when what he wanted to do was ease Tia into his arms. She must have been devastated. Obviously the rejection still hurt. Likely it had colored her whole outlook on life. Sure, children were resilient, but how did someone bounce back from this?

Dear God, and now he had to tell her that Grant had changed his mind about marrying her. What would *that* rejection do to her? "Why did the couple adopt someone else?"

"I was never told."

Mac glanced sharply at her. She might not have been told, but he'd swear she now knew or suspected the reason. He also sensed it was a closed subject. He switched lanes again, getting ready to exit the freeway. Let her have her secrets. And her pride. If she ever wanted him to know, she'd tell him. He was more concerned at the moment with how she'd deal with Grant's rejection. "That must have been rough on you."

"I don't suppose it was all that bad. The Bowens were kind and easy to live with. They provided a roof over my head, clothes, a clean environment."

"Did you only live with the one family?"

"Yes."

"Isn't that unusual?" He drove down the exit ramp and stopped at a red light.

"I guess. But after the adoption fell through, I decided if I was very, very good, maybe someone else would want me. Or at the very least, the Bowens would learn to love me. Silly, huh?"

"I don't think it was silly." The light turned green. "You were just a kid."

"True. I didn't understand then that Molly loved me as much as she allowed herself to love any of her foster kids. But she always knew they weren't hers. I realize now she gave all she could. I just wanted more."

More. He could relate to that. "I suppose Grant told you our folks were divorced when we were ten?"

"Yes."

"Did he also tell you we each spent every other summer with our dad? He wouldn't take us both at once. Dad decided early on that Grant took after him more than I did. And from about age seven on, Grant spent every summer with Dad, while I stayed home with Mom. The rejection and being separated from Grant for three long months at a stretch...whew, it really shredded my self-confidence."

She made a sympathetic murmur.

He maneuvered the road a tad faster than necessary. "Grant, on the other hand, always arrived at our Labor Day reunions more cocksure than when we'd parted."

She sighed. "How like Grant."

"Yes." Mac smiled, but it wasn't a pleasant memory. As a result of their forced separation, he'd became shier around the opposite sex, while Grant had become bolder. Mac might not understand the rejection Tia had felt as a little girl, but he knew the devastating sensation of feeling unwanted.

His two attempts at making love had taught him that ugly lesson.

He turned toward Southcenter shopping mall, shoving his old wounds back into their cubbyhole. His childhood woes didn't matter. But Tia's did. How did she see herself based on those old views? Had she hardened herself against rejection? Or would she be devastated when he told her Grant had been about to break up with her? That he had chosen someone else over her? Mac groaned inwardly. If only he could put off telling her altogether. But then Gwen would take matters into her own hands. No. Tia needed to hear this from him. An unpleasant warmth layered his belly.

He pulled into the parking lot of the five-story building where Grant's business, Quell Inc., had its offices. He parked in the spot reserved for Grant's car, shut off the engine and turned to face his brother's fiancée. As Tia glanced at him, he recalled the kiss they'd shared, the abandon she'd displayed, the hunger he'd tasted.

For a long moment passion thickened in his veins. And then a horrible truth struck him, washing his heated blood cold. When he told Tia about Grant and Gwen, what if she didn't believe him? What if she thought he was trying to further his own case to win her?

The ache in his head throbbed. This news could wait. He opened his door. Rain pelted his face. He welcomed its soothing chill against his fevered flesh. Tucking the keys into his hand, he raced toward the front door of the office building. Tia arrived under the shelter of the portico a second later.

Wet droplets pearled her thick ebony lashes, curled the soft raven hair at her temples. She was so beautiful he could hardly look at her without aching to touch her. If he lived to be a hundred, he'd never understand why his brother cheated on Tia with Gwen Gallagher. How long had it been going on? And how the hell was he supposed to avoid Gwen and keep his business running toward the launch?

He searched for the right keys. Finding them, he felt something odd against his palm. "Funny, these two keys feel waxy."

"Waxy?"

"Yeah." He lifted them toward the overhead light. A white residue edged the side of one key. He sniffed it. "That's weird. It smells like...soap."

She frowned. "That is weird. Maybe Grant dropped the keys in the bathroom near the sink."

"I guess. That must be what happened." But it felt more to him like the keys had sat in a bar of soap. Shrugging off the oddity, Mac opened both locks protecting the front entrance, worked the security code, then secured everything again once they were inside. The building was three months old and retained that fresh-paint, new-carpet scent. They stood in a wide open space that sported tall plants against taller windows. The only concession to the season was a large fir tree, lavished with gold and silver balls and bows. The golden angel at its tip brushed the eight-foot ceiling.

Although Tia thought it beautiful, it did nothing to inspire any holiday spirit in her. Inexplicably a shiver tracked down her spine. She preferred this building during the day. Now it had an abandoned feeling. Like the one deep within her heart.

She glanced at the glass walls of the realty office that occupied the largest portion of this floor and stood like a dark fortress to their right. She saw her reflection, obscured and somehow looking like the sorry little girl no one had wanted. She couldn't believe she'd confided in Mac. She hadn't told Grant about almost being adopted when she was eight.

What was there about Mac that made her open up, share her private pain? Trust him with such personal knowledge?

She shook herself, pushing away the questions, the lifelong heartache and the ugly memories. She needed to concentrate on finding Grant's killer. Nothing more. She glanced around and saw that Mac had moved ahead.

The only illumination came from six overhead recessed lights. The dim glow cast shadows across the marble steps leading to twin elevators and gave her the impression there were evildoers hiding in every corner. With her nerves twitching, she hastened to keep up with Mac's long strides.

Quell Inc. was on the fifth floor. They rode up in silence. The doors slid open to a short hallway leading to the private-investigations offices. Mac found the correct key, noticing that it also had an odd waxy feel.

Tia glanced right and left, half expecting someone to leap out at them. Quell had a separate security system. Mac worked the sequence of numbers. He held the door open for Tia to enter first.

The reception area reflected a business operating well in the black. In tones of burgundy and aqua, the area was dominated by leather and oak. Someone had strung red and green garlands and taped holiday cards to a file cabinet. A live, decorated Douglas fir with a silver star on top reposed in one corner. The air held the rich scent of pine. Tia glanced at Mac and wondered if his Christmas memories were happy ones. Or if his parents' divorce had somehow evoked the need in him to bring some happiness to sad and lonely children.

In the huge scheme of things, did the reason matter? Just the fact that he devoted himself to finding and developing toys that enriched the lives of little kids deepened her fondness for Mac. He was the kind of man she wished had fathered her. He was the kind of man she wanted to father her children. But that would never be. She had no right even to think it.

She caught a warm glance from Mac and fought the urge to offer him a look as warm. Encouraging the blossoming love inside herself for this man was dangerous. Foolhardy. It would only lead to heartache. For them both.

She forced her gaze from his, glanced around again. Grant and his partner employed two operatives and one office manager, who handled everything from accounts to letter writing. Beyond her desk, a hall led to three other offices. The two operatives shared the first office, and at the end of the hall, Grant and his partner's private domains stood across from each other.

"Feels eerie in here." Tia shivered inside her rain-damp coat. She didn't like being in commercial buildings at night, without all the hustle and bustle of the workday, when shadows lived and silence reigned. She struggled against the unpleasant sensation. "Gives me the willies."

"I usually like the quiet," Mac said as they started down the hall. "Makes it easier to think."

He looked like a man with a lot on his mind. She wondered for the hundredth time what he was keeping from her. But for some reason she couldn't bring herself to push the point.

They opened Grant's door. A tinny voice rang out. Mac rammed his arm against Tia's middle. "Stay back."

Her pulse jumped. He switched on the light. Tia gasped. File cabinets had been overturned, the desk littered with papers and computer disks. The telephone lay on the floor, the source of the disembodied voice. He took a step forward.

She caught his arm. Her nerves quaked. "Mac, don't. Whoever did this might still be here."

"No. There's no place to hide. Go to the front desk and call 911. I'll start the computer and print out the information before the police arrive."

"Okay." Tia raced down the hall to the reception area. Her heart banged against her ribs. She grasped the phone. It was on the line connected to Grant's office. The operator informed her, if she wanted to make a call, she should hang up and try again. She punched another line. A dial tone filled her ear. With a trembling hand, she poked the 9.

A footstep sounded behind her. She whipped around. A shiny object descended toward her head. She yelped. Lurched to the side. But the object found its mark. Pain crashed through her skull. The room spun. Her knees buckled. As she dropped to the floor, her vision blurring, she spied a wavy figure, dressed like a skier in mourning, scoot out the door. Then all turned black.

"TIA." MAC CALLED HER back to consciousness. She pried her eyes open. His face hovered above her. Blurred in, then out, then in again. She lifted her hand toward him, realizing his eyes were filled with horror and alarm. She moaned softly. Her hand shifted, going, instead, to her own aching forehead. To where Mac had his hankie pressed. "He was here. Whoever did that to Grant's office—he hit me with something."

"The silver star from the Christmas tree. Are you okay?"

"I think so." She realized the fingers she'd put to her head were sticky. She looked at them. "I'm bleeding."

"I know. Hold this on the wound." He pressed her hand onto the hankie at her forehead. It felt damp.

"Can you stand?" He began helping her to her feet. "Walk?"

"Of course." She held the hankie in place and struggled to her feet, feeling slightly nauseated and mentally numb, as though it weren't *her* forehead that had been stabbed by the treetop ornament.

"I've got to get you out of here. Somewhere safe. Whoever did this might still be on the premises."

"No. He ran out."

"It was a man, then?" His brows shot up. "Did you see him?"

"No. Only an image. Blurry. Don't know if it was a man or a woman." She stepped from his grasp. The room spun once, then leveled. "We need that information, Mac."

"You need a hospital and that's where we're going. Now." There was such guilt in his eyes she wanted to reach up and touch his cheek. But she hadn't the strength.

Mac said, "This is all my fault. I should never have dragged you into this danger. After the hospital I'm taking you home and you're going to stay out of this mess."

"Like hell I am." Tia felt as though she'd been struck again. "I'm in this for the long haul. Especially after being attacked."

"No." Mac touched her cheek. "I don't want anything to happen to you."

"Neither do I." She stuck out her chin, thinking

she probably looked fairly silly holding a cloth to her head, with blood staining her face and clothes. "And the best way to insure that is to find out who our nemesis is."

Mac shook his head.

She made a face. "I don't feel well enough to argue about this right now. Whoever was here, whoever did that to Grant's office, might have been after the same thing we are."

"I don't like the look of that gash." He peered at her forehead. "You're still bleeding. You probably need some stitches. A doctor should tend to it right now."

"Heads always bleed a lot. But I'll let you take me to the hospital *after* we get what we came for." She stood her ground, refusing to budge. "Did you find it in the computer?"

"Not yet." His eyes still swam with guilt. And concern. "I found the file, but it's password protected."

"Then we'll have to figure it out." She skirted past Mac, holding the hankie secure, and hurried toward Grant's office. "Come on. We're wasting time."

Mac sat in Grant's chair. Tia leaned over his shoulder, breathing in his special scent that was now a mixture of his brother's aftershave and Mac's own special smell. It made her light-headed. Made her yearn for more from him than he could give, than she had any right to want.

He began trying words to find the one that would open the file they sought. He started with "Tia." It didn't work.

She suggested, "Coy Toys?"

He typed it. "Nope."

He tried "Gwen."

Wrong again.

Tia frowned. Why in the world would Grant use the name "Gwen" for a password, unless he suspected *she* was the one who'd betrayed Mac? Were they onto something? Should he try all the employees?

Before she could ask, he typed "Holly."

Wrong.

"Holly Beary?"

Wrong.

Tia pressed the cloth to her wound, wincing at the sharp pain, but the bleeding seemed to have abated. "Bear?"

His fingers flew across the keyboard. "No." He blew out a frustrated breath.

"Teddy?"

"No."

"Teddy bear?"

"Nope." He ground his teeth. "This isn't going to work. The computer will shut us out after another couple of tries."

Tia strained to think of something else. Her head pounded and her vision doubled. Then cleared. "How about your birthday?"

"Too obvious," Mac groused. But he had no other suggestion, so punched in the numbers.

"Bingo," Tia cried as the file opened. But her delight fled as quickly as it had come. The screen that appeared bore the heading: Coy Toys Employees. But the rest of the file was blank. "It's been erased?"

"Yes." Mac swore. "Whoever just knocked you down beat us to this file."

Tia glanced at the pile of disks on Grant's desk. "Grant would have made a backup disk."

They quickly checked every disk. Then again slowly. Mac scowled, climbing to his feet, fury on his face. "If he made one, it's gone now."

Disappointment dropped over Tia. Her head was beginning to thump. "What I don't understand is how he or she got in here. I mean, the doors were locked, not jimmied or anything."

Mac shrugged, then she saw a dawning glint in his eyes. He snapped his fingers. "The residue on the keys. Someone must have gotten hold of Grant's keys and pressed them into a bar of soap, then had copies made."

"Can that be done?"

Mac nodded. "I saw it on one of those detective shows once. 'Murder She Wrote,' I think."

Fear shot through Tia. "Dear God, Mac. Why would someone do that unless they knew what Grant was up to?"

His eyes rounded. "You mean, whoever sold the blueprints of my Holly Beary to Lei Industries knew Grant was investigating?"

"It's the only explanation."

His face paled as the full significance hit him. "If you're right, then he or she must have known we traded places."

She held her head in both hands and nodded, too horror-stricken to speak.

Mac stood up, shaking his head. "But...but that would mean he or she meant to kill Grant, not me."

Chapter Nine

Mac's face was the color of fresh snow, his eyes wide with shock. He appeared to be swallowing a lump of coal. Tia stepped toward him, automatically reaching out, touching his arm, offering comfort as he'd offered it to her minutes ago.

He held himself as stiff as a stone sculpture. "If Grant was the intended victim…"

His voice broke. His gaze met hers, the turquoise bright as though heated from a fire behind, a fire fed by impotent rage and confusion. If ever she understood how someone was feeling, it was this man, at this time.

She finished his thought for him. "Then the killer knows you're impersonating Grant."

He nodded, then jammed his hands through his short hair. Anger spewed from him in one curse after another. His outburst ended as abruptly as it began. He looked as though he were shaking off some evil spell, as though he couldn't believe his own behavior. The tips of his ears glowed pink, and he wore a sheepish, apologetic expression. "I'm sorry, I don't usually swear like that."

"I know." She squeezed his forearm. His eyes

cooled, but retained a warmth that came from deep within, that had the power to reach inside and touch her soul. A whisper of fire shimmied through Tia, electrified her, terrified her. She released him and stepped back with sudden self-consciousness.

Gingerly readjusting the cloth on her wound, she said, "I can't imagine which of our suspects is responsible. I would swear they all believed you were Grant. I suppose that just means one of them is a really good actor."

Mac thought about Gwen. "One of them wasn't acting. *She* thought I *was* Grant."

"Nancy?"

"No." He turned off the computer and moved away from the desk. "I want to get you to a hospital, but first we'd better call the police and report this break-in."

She shook her head, instantly regretting it as the room began to whirl. "We can't do that, Mac. We need to lock this office and get out of here. Let Grant's staff discover the burglary."

"What?" He was incredulous, obviously recalling her insistence last night that he call the cops and tell them about Grant.

Tia took his hand, shutting her heart to the instant unspoken connection she felt. "If we talk to the police, we'll have to explain our suspicions. Without proof, we'll sound like *we're* doing something dishonest."

"You don't know that."

"True, but if by some remote chance the police do believe us, they'll stop your launch with their own investigation so fast your head will spin."

Mac considered this. He narrowed his eyes. "I think that's what the killer is counting on."

"Exactly." Another thought struck her, chilling her. "Oh, my God, Mac. Even if we don't report the break-in, as Grant, you'll be required to show up here as soon as the police are called in."

His eyes widened with understanding. "So either way, Grant's killer diverts my attention from the launch and I'm defeated."

He looked beaten, but she realized it was fatigue and stress more than anything. Mac Coy was a fighter. He wouldn't go down without one hell of a struggle.

Tia released a heavy breath. "Well, we'll just have to show our opponent we aren't that easily done in."

He nodded, giving her a wry smile, then leaned over and righted the file cabinets. She rushed to help him replace the spilled files. Within fifteen minutes they had Grant's office looking presentable, undisturbed. As long as no one dug too closely into the files or the desk drawers for a few days, there would be no alarm raised.

They shut off the light and closed Grant's door. The door to the operative's office stood ajar, another reminder of the intruder. Mac peeked inside. All seemed in order. He pulled the door closed, then caught Tia by the arm. Putting Grant's office to rights seemed to have drained the last of her energy. Her lush mouth was pinched at the corners, and her eyes had dark smudges beneath them. She looked as though her head was pounding worse than his own.

"It's time we had that cut examined." Mac managed to keep the worry out of his voice as he led her to the reception area. She wasn't bleeding anymore, but as sleepy as she appeared, he worried she had a concussion. Dammit, he shouldn't have dragged her into this mess. "One more thing."

He sat Tia in a leather chair, then grabbed a tissue from the box on the desk, wiped the blood off the silver star and put it back on the tree. He gave the office one last glance. Satisfied, he helped Tia to her feet, then locked the door.

Tia leaned on him. Moving haltingly, like drunken lovers, he helped her into the elevator. She didn't pull away, just nestled against him as though she belonged there. Mac dismissed the fanciful thought, but he couldn't dismiss the longing, the yearning. Would he ever find a woman to call his own, someone who wanted the real Mac Coy, not some imitation of his brother?

The lobby was eerily quiet as they emerged from the elevator. His every muscle tensed, alert to danger. The dim lights threw ominous shadows in all directions. He hastened Tia to the outside door. It was unlocked.

His heart climbed his throat. Was the burglar lurking just outside? With perhaps a gun? Had he or she done something to the Porsche? A pulse pounded at his temple. He secured the main office door. "Stay here a moment."

Tia huddled under the portico, out of the downpour, looking small and vulnerable and needy. If only she needed him. Mac squashed the thought. She needed Grant, and he couldn't give her that. He rushed to the Porsche. Rain fell in heavy sheets, soaking the Armani suit. He unlocked the car and found a flashlight. First he scanned the shrubs surrounding the parking lot. But no one appeared to be hiding there. Next, as best he could, he checked the Porsche for anything that looked amiss. Finding nothing, he motioned for Tia to join him. "Okay. It's safe."

Once they were tucked in the car cruising down the freeway, Tia asked, "Where are we going?"

"Valley General."

"And after that?"

"Back to Grant's to sleep."

"But we need to go to the plant and collect the personnel files."

"We can do that first thing in the morning."

"What if our burglar beats us to it?"

"If he or she wanted those personnel files, they will already be missing."

"Oh," she moaned softly. "That will really tick me off."

He chuckled. "I appreciate the sentiment, but if they *are* gone, we'll find another way. I'll be damned if the person who killed my brother is going to get away with it. Whichever of my trusted six betrayed me and murdered Grant will pay for it in spades."

MAC DROVE STRAIGHT to Valley General and helped Tia into the emergency room. Her wound was cleaned and tended. The gash required four stitches. The doctor diagnosed a slight concussion, recommended Tylenol and prescribed bed rest.

Mac drove her to Grant's condo and retrieved her bag from the back seat. He scanned the parking area, then hurried Tia up the walk. A creeping sensation of being watched made him move faster than normal. The cheery wreath on the door played "Silent Night" as they approached, resounding with bold clarity, drawing attention to them, adding to his jitters.

Quickly he worked the security pad, grateful Grant

had installed a state-of-the-art alarm system here. If nothing else they could sleep without worry of being attacked in their beds.

The condo was chilly, but the air held the sweet scent of fresh pine. He made a mental note to water the Christmas tree and raised the thermostat. In his concern for Tia, he had hardly noticed his own discomfort. But now his damp clothes felt clammy against his fatigued flesh. He wanted nothing more than to strip and stand beneath a hot shower for ten minutes. But if he felt this bad, Tia must feel worse. "Why don't you take a hot bath before bed?"

She was shivering. "I don't think I have the strength."

He found her a towel, then carried her bag to the bedroom. "Go get into a robe and I'll run the water for you. It will ease the chill from your bones and you'll sleep better."

She nodded. "Okay. Thanks."

He took a towel of his own and peeled off the ruined suit coat, then the shirt and tie. As steamy water filled the tub, he buffed his hair, then his upper body with the soft terry cloth. The events of the past forty-eight hours had his head feeling like *he'd* been hit with the silver star.

Tia appeared in the doorway in a soft pink robe and fuzzy slippers. Her hair was pinned up off her neck. She looked innocent and vulnerable, beautiful and touchable. He swallowed the urge to reach out and caress that milky spot in the hollow of her neck. His body ached from fatigue and stress, and a need that would not be fulfilled.

He excused himself and left her to the bathroom. In Grant's room he exchanged his damp slacks for sweats. Tia's discarded clothes lay on the carpet, feminine undergarments, all lacy and red, topping the heap like a cherry on an ice-cream sundae. His male imagination revved into high gear, running wild and free, sending hot jabs of desire straight to his groin.

He groaned softly and forced himself to move. He found a blanket and pillow in the linen closet and made himself a bed on the sofa. It was wide and deep-cushioned, long enough for him to sleep comfortably on most nights. As tired as he was tonight, it would feel like a feather bed.

He plopped down on it, figuring he'd warm up and drift right off to sleep, but his mind betrayed him, conjuring up one fantasy after another about the woman bathing down the hall. He got up, checked all the windows and doors.

Tia emerged from the bathroom, looking once more like the angel on top of Grant's tree. He squashed the images that threatened to overwhelm him again, even as her delicate scent assaulted his resolve. "The condo is locked up tight and the alarm's activated. So you can sleep without worry."

"I think I will." She yawned, covering her mouth as though embarrassed by this natural act. He found it alluring. Distracting. Enticing.

"I'll see you in the morning, then." His voice was raspy. "I want to get to the plant early."

He waited until she closed the bedroom door, then headed into the shower. Standing under the hot water, all he could think of was climbing into that bed with Tia. He turned the spigot to cold. Half an hour later he was on the sofa, deep in a hard, dreamless slumber.

He had no idea how long he slept before her scream woke him.

TIA TRIED TO SCREAM again. Again no sound emitted from her rounded lips. Terror ripped through her. He had her, gripping her upper arms in his painful grasp. She wrenched this way and that. But she couldn't break free.

"Tia. Tia, wake up."

Tia came awake slowly as though she was buried under layers of gauze. She could still feel his grip on her arms. Why? Her eyes felt gummy, pasted shut. She pried them open. No monster from her past, just the sweet face of Mac Coy.

His arresting features were fixed in a mask of fear. "It was a nightmare, baby. That's all. You're okay. I won't let anything happen to you."

Oh, how she wanted to believe him.

He pulled her against his bare chest. She was so glad for the solace, so hungry for it, she nuzzled her cheek to his naked flesh, her ear nestled against his sternum. His heart beat fast, as though he'd been as frightened as she. Which was impossible. He couldn't know the horror of her dream.

Mac rubbed her back through the T-shirt she slept in, his fingers moving in gentle, soothing strokes. "It'll be okay."

She wanted to believe him, but he didn't have all the facts. His assurances were well meant. And appreciated. But her nightmares weren't dreams. They were reality in the world of Tia Larken.

As the quiet moments passed, neither she nor Mac trying to separate, Tia realized her pulse was gradually humming faster, her fears, her anxiety diluting into something sweet and pure and forbidden. She felt it in the pressure of Mac's fingertips on her back, in the thrum of his heart against her ear, in the blood rushing through her veins with sizzle and promise.

She lifted her head and found him gazing down at her. His turquoise eyes were three shades darker, need standing bold and fresh in their depths. She reached a finger to trace his mouth, to touch his cleft chin. There was something so innocent about this man, something so unlike his twin, it erased the similarities. She didn't look at Mac and see Grant. She saw only Mac, as though she'd known his brother in some distant lifetime, a long-forgotten childhood.

Mac lowered his mouth to hers. She didn't pull back but strained her neck, raising her mouth to meet his. The kiss sent ribbons of passion floating through her, soft and silken, heating her blood with scintillating bliss. He moved hesitantly, as though he wasn't sure of himself…or of her. She twisted in his arms, put her hands behind his neck and pulled him closer, letting him know she wanted this as much as he did.

More.

He moaned, a low hungry growl of pleasure, and wrapped his arms around her like a man overcome, like a beggar presented with a million dollars, a chocoholic locked in a candy factory. He deepened the kiss with unexpected speed. His tongue danced with hers, partners in a tango as old as time itself, each stroke in unison, each dip and plunge in step, teasing, tantalizing, erotic.

Heat coursed through her veins, pooled in her belly and lower. She knew she should stop this now, before it went any further, before Mac lost himself in this wild passion. He would regret it. But his hand was moving over her back again, sending her senses packing. Her body ignored her will, giving itself over to the feel of his hands slipping beneath her shirt, feathering up her sides, then finding her taut nipples.

Pleasure dragged his name from her parted lips. "Oh, Mac. Oh, Mac."

He tensed as though she'd called him some other name, as though she'd called him...Grant. He pulled his hands from beneath her shirt, setting her away from him. He was breathless, his eyes glazed with desire, his face flushed from their kisses. But his expression was edged with alarm. She half expected to see guilt or some form of confusion, but she saw something else. Fear.

Was he afraid of her? Or of himself?

"I can't do this." He struggled up and off the bed. His plaintive cry might have meant he was impotent and therefore incapable of actually making love with her. But she'd felt his need for her the second she'd pressed her body full to his. He wasn't a man physically incapable of sex. His reticence had to be emotional.

It must be her he didn't want. The old hurt slashed through her, tearing her heart apart, leaving a gaping wound that couldn't be repaired with stitches. That would never heal. How could she have let this happen? Why, despite all wisdom to the contrary, had she even dared hope Mac would want her?

Her throat thickened with tears. She understood without his telling her that Grant stood between them. He would always be between them. She hugged her knees to her chest. She could barely breathe for need of Mac. Barely make her pulse slow down. But as much as she wanted his love, she was glad Mac had instinctively known she was wrong for him. Loving her would only mess up his whole life.

Even so, at this moment, she feared loneliness most of all. "Mac, please, don't leave. Would you…could you stay and just…just hold me until I fall asleep again?"

He looked as though she'd asked him to plunge a knife into his heart. For a heavy moment he stared at her, a man torn between running for his life and staying to help a woman he cared deeply for. She didn't want to play on his sympathies. Whatever desire he felt for her was likely just a confused bonding because of their grief over Grant. Theirs was a complicated relationship. And in five days it would end. They would go their separate ways.

She would survive. He would be better off with Tia Larken out of his life. But right now, at this moment, she needed him—and he needed her, too. What was wrong with that? What was wrong with their holding on to each other, making these next few days easier for each other?

"I…I'm sorry." He looked distraught, distressed. "I can't."

MAC STOOD ON THE DECK staring out at the black beneath that was Lake Washington. The rain had stopped. The steady dripping of a downspout was the only noise in the silence of the early morning. He breathed in the crisp, fresh air, felt it embracing his fevered flesh, cooling his ardor.

"Ah, Grant," he said with regret and sorrow clogging his throat. Would he ever feel whole again without his twin? His chest squeezed with pain. There were so many things he wanted to ask Grant. So many things he was finding out that made no sense, that made him question how well he'd known his brother.

He rubbed his bristled jaw. At least he no longer felt the heavy disloyalty over Tia he'd suffered twenty-four hours ago—not since learning about Grant and Gwen.

But that didn't give him the right to force his affections on Tia. He'd only meant to comfort her. But he was weak in every way a man could be. He'd taken advantage of the situation. He hated himself for that. He'd heard that people often make love in the wake of grief. Heard it was some sort of affirmation of life. He supposed that explained Tia's participation.

But he'd had no such noble thoughts. He'd wanted her, plain and simple. Wanted her so badly still, he couldn't bring himself to walk back into the condo.

God, he was a fool. If he hadn't called a halt to it when he had, he wouldn't have been able to stop. How could he even consider making love to Tia in Grant's bed? A bed the two of them had shared on numerous occasions? Ardor released its fierce grip on him.

How could he even consider making love to Tia after his miserable experiences? The thought of those other women, his too-quick responses, stripped the last of the heat from his blood. What if *that* had happened with Tia? He shuddered. He couldn't bear it if he'd embarrassed himself with the only woman he'd ever loved. He couldn't bear it if Tia laughed at him.

He moved back inside, locking the glass door behind him. He settled on the sofa. Half an hour later he was still wide awake. He gathered his blanket and pillow and walked to Grant's bedroom. The door stood ajar. He called Tia's name softly. No answer.

He stepped into the room. Her gentle, even breathing told him she was asleep. As gingerly as possible, he placed his pillow next to hers, stretched his blanket over the spread and lay down beside her, draping an arm around her waist.

She sighed contentedly as though comforted by his presence even as she slept. He feared this was a dangerous mistake, doubted he'd be able to fall back to sleep, guessed he'd be back on the deck in minutes. But for some reason just touching Tia, even through the barrier of the blankets, calmed his worries, sweetened his thoughts and eased him into dreamland.

THE AROMA OF FRESH COFFEE and the absence of the reassuring pressure she'd felt throughout the night awakened Tia. It was still dark in Grant's bedroom. She struggled upright, stretching, and switched on the bedside lamp. Four-thirty. When Mac said he wanted to be at the plant early, he wasn't kidding.

A slight ache tapped her temples. She frowned, eliciting a tightening on her forehead. Memory zinged through her. The attack in Grant's office, the stitches. She squeezed her eyes shut, conjuring up the image of the person who'd struck her, but it was no clearer than it had been last night.

Frustrated, she sat straighter and discovered her body felt as sore and tender as her wound. Less than eight hours of sack time did that to her. Some of that great-smelling coffee would fix all that ailed her physically, but nothing could mend her mental agony.

As she stepped from the bed, she spotted Mac's pillow and blanket beside her. A smile crossed her lips, warming her inside and out, although she'd have thought nothing could do that. She'd underestimated Mac. Completely. She'd have sworn he wouldn't step foot in this room again—as long as she occupied this bed. But determined as he'd been not to stay with her, he'd done it, anyway. Her smile widened, the warm feeling raising her spirits. What had changed his mind?

She quickly dressed in fresh jeans and a sweater that featured snowmen cavorting on skis. She brushed her hair, applied a minimum of makeup and wandered toward the kitchen. A woman's voice stopped her in the hall. Did Mac have company? At a quarter to five in the morning? She crept closer, straining to make out what was being said, and realized he was listening to an answering machine.

"Grant, are you there? Pick up if you are," the woman pleaded. The voice sounded familiar, but Tia couldn't place it. Where had she heard it? Recently? "I'll come over if you like. I really need you right now. I know you must need me, too. Or is 'Ms. Coffee, Tea or Me' still holding your hand? Really, Grant. You have to tell her."

Shock stole through Tia. This woman sounded as if she was more to Grant than a concerned friend. She heard Mac swear and realized he knew this woman and what her involvement with Grant was. Tia padded into the kitchen. "Tell me what?"

Mac leaped a foot in the air. He lurched around, his eyes wide, a trapped expression on his cleanly shaven face. He'd had the answering machine volume turned low, apparently thinking only he could hear it. A notepad and pen rested beside a mug of coffee. He'd been writing down the messages.

"What are you doing?"

Mac licked his lips. "Weeding out what needs to be handled now from the stuff that can be put off until after the toy is launched."

She nodded toward the answering machine. "Which category does that woman fit?"

He sputtered, "I—I, er…"

She scowled at him. "Who was that, Mac? And don't bother lying—I know you know."

He grimaced. "Gwen."

"Gwen?" The name meant nothing to Tia. Then she realized she did know a Gwen. Had met her yesterday. "Gwen Gallagher?"

He nodded.

"Coy Toy's vice president, Gwen?"

He nodded again.

Her mouth dried. "What did she want to talk to you alone about yesterday, 'Grant'?"

"I was going to tell you."

"Tell me now."

He looked like it was the last thing he wanted to do. But she would not be put off. She walked to the coffeemaker and poured herself a full mug, then turned to face him.

The tips of his ears were pink. Whatever he knew, it made him damned uncomfortable. But this was the man who'd held her through the night, who'd kept her nightmares at bay. She trusted him as she trusted no other man. "I'm a big girl, Mac. I can handle whatever it is."

"I, er, it took me by surprise. I swear I didn't know anything about it."

She leaned back against the counter. "About what?"

"Gwen and…and Grant."

"Gwen and Grant?" What was he saying? No. It couldn't be. Could it? "Are you telling me Gwen and Grant were lovers?"

He swallowed hard and started waving his hands. "All I know is the minute you were out of the lab, she leaped at me. I was stunned. Last I knew she was living with a guy who worked for Technosoft, so at first I just thought she was spewing out grief at 'my' death. But whoa, was I wrong."

Tia eyed him speculatively, surprise gripping her insides, boggling her mind and releasing a wedge of memory from the previous night. "Gwen is the one you're sure believes you're Grant."

"Yes."

"And...?"

"And I still think she does."

"Why?"

He blew out a huge breath. "She insisted she was tired of hiding 'our' relationship."

"Did you remind her that 'you' were engaged to me?"

He chuckled, a mirthless little sound, and the tips of his ears were Santa-suit red. "Er, she asked when 'I' was going to break off the engagement. Actually she said if 'I' didn't tell you, she would."

So, her feeling that Grant was pulling away from her was not imagined. She recalled the message about the talk he'd wanted to have with her. Tia sank to the bar stool with a thud. This was the funniest thing she'd heard in weeks. Here she'd been so concerned about breaking up with Grant, and he'd been about to break up with her. She started to laugh.

Mac frowned at her so hard his eyebrows bent into arcs. "What are you laughing at?"

She stopped and rolled her neck. The muscles felt knotted. "Life and its jokes on me. Oh, don't look so sad. This isn't the end of my world. But it may mean the end of my involvement in your launch.''

''No.'' He shook his head, the fear she'd seen two nights ago standing in his eyes. If she deserted him now, he'd be all alone with no one to trust.

But what choice did she have? ''I may have to, Mac. Gwen could be a real problem otherwise. What are you going to tell her if I show up with you every day for the next few days?''

He drank his coffee, mulling over ideas. ''I'll tell her I'll break off with you as soon as Holly Beary is launched.''

''From the sound of it—'' Tia pointed to the answering machine again ''—that won't make her too happy.''

''Tough,'' he said confidently, but his certainty faltered as he contemplated the encounter. ''I'll make her see. Somehow.''

Misery crept into his eyes, and she knew he dreaded the confrontation with Gwen. She touched his hand reassuringly. ''If it makes you feel any better, I'm not looking forward to running into her now, either.''

He smiled wryly. ''Are you hungry? Grant has an array of cold cereal and fresh milk, but not much else.''

''Sure. If Gwen decides to challenge my right to 'you' even after you call her off, then I'd rather not face her on coffee alone.''

BUD GIBSON'S WAS the lone car in the lot when they parked in Mac's spot at the plant. Tia made a mental note to call Ginny this morning and arrange a get-together.

They ascended in Mac's private elevator as they had yesterday. The third floor was as quiet as a tomb. A shiver crept down Tia's spine. She stepped closer to Mac. She hadn't thought the attack last night had affected her much. She realized now she was wrong. She didn't suppose anyone came away from something like that without feeling vulnerable, and anger bloomed inside her.

Mac unlocked his office, crossed to his desk and called Bud. He told the guard they were in the building, asked if all was secure, smiled at the answer and hung up. He said, "So far, so good. We made it through the night without any incidents or disasters."

"Hopefully our nemesis limited his or her damages to Grant's office."

"From your lips to God's ears." He retrieved the ring of master keys from his desk. Automatically he checked them for any soapy residue, but found none. "I don't like creeping around my people's offices."

She shrugged. "Desperate times…"

"Exactly."

Tia followed Mac to Nancy's office next door. "When I started this company, it was just Gwen and me. I acquired the others one at a time, as the need for their services arose. Grant was right. I believed everything they told me. Didn't verify anyone's references."

"We'll do that now."

"*If* the records are intact so we can."

They unlocked Nancy's office. The personnel files were in a locked drawer of a tall metal filing cabinet. They found the key in her desk. In an unlocked drawer.

"So much for security." Mac shook his head,

wearing a look of disgust. Worry had his mouth thinned, his jaw set. He opened the drawer, seeming braced for anything. A second later she saw his shoulders slump. "They're here."

He opened each folder, quickly rifling the papers inside them. "All the pages seem to be right, too."

"Good." She let out her own tightly held breath. "Now what?"

"To the copy room." He pulled the files free and led her down the hall. After checking the machine for paper, they began copying the contents of one folder at a time. As soon as one was complete, Mac returned the folder to the cabinet drawer, while Tia placed the copied pages into a huge envelope. It was taking longer than they'd expected. Daylight began filtering into the room.

Tia's nerves felt as tight as Christmas-ball hooks. The employees would be arriving soon. Would they get caught at this? By the wrong person? As if on cue, she heard the main elevator open. Tia's heart skipped a beat.

Mac appeared in the copy-room doorway. "It's Will."

"All done here." Tia's nerves jostled. She gathered the last sheet and pulled the original from the copier. She handed Mac the closed file and added the copies to the envelope. Scurrying like thieves in the night, they returned the last folder, then relocked Nancy's office door.

Will Holden's scream resounded down the hall.

Chapter Ten

Tia and Mac raced down the hall to the end room.

"They're ruined!" Will shrieked. "Ruined!"

Tia held the precious envelope to her thundering heart. She scanned the office, noting the array of Christmas decorations, all in shades of pink—from the flocked tree to the tiny twinkling lights strung around the walls to the foil bows. She tried to pinpoint the source of Will Holden's distress.

This area had a skylight over an artist's table and several display easels, each holding what had clearly been a presentation for Holly Beary. Neon paint obliterated the images, the sales messages. Someone had sprayed them in what appeared to have been a vicious fit of rage.

"Look! Look at this...this abomination!" Will's arm poked the air like an orchestra leader's baton. His narrow face was the color of his tree.

"Damned vandals. They've destroyed the scans of photos, the page layouts, the point-of-purchase displays. Even the counter cards." He lifted sheets of paper and let them flutter to the floor like the stuffing from a piñata. "What kind of security have we got in this place, for God's sake, that someone could walk into a man's private domain and destroy his work?''

Mac strode to Will's desk. ''I'll get the security guard right up here and find out.''

Mac lifted the telephone receiver.

Will gasped, reared back in horror, then lunged toward Mac. ''No. Don't touch anything. The police will want to dust for fingerprints.''

Mac kept dialing.

Will shook his head, his artificially gold hair waving slightly. Disbelief widened his gray eyes to the size of billiard balls. ''What kind of detective are you that you don't know that?''

Mac blanched, but managed to keep his voice level. ''We aren't calling the police, Mr. Holden.''

''What?'' Will looked ready to explode. ''Why not?''

''Because the police would swarm all over your office. They'd spread fingerprint powder. They'd check every corner, every crevice.''

Will nodded vigorously. ''Yes, yes, yes.''

Mac shook his head. ''No, no, no. *That* would only serve to keep you from reconstructing your ad campaign. Which needs to be done by the end of the day.''

Will's eyebrows shot skyward. ''By the end of the day?''

''Today.''

The head of publicity planted his hands on his hips. ''How am I supposed to do that?''

Mac gave him a tolerant grin. ''Surely the master copies are at the printers.''

''Well, yes…but—''

''Then you'll need to get over there, get them reproduced. Then bring them back here and repackage and mail them today.''

''Have you any idea of the time involved?''

''Yes. That's why I can't have the police costing you a day's work. Not with the wages I'm paying you.''

Tia bit back a smile, but Will found nothing funny in the situation. He sputtered so hard she wondered if he'd destroyed the artwork himself. ''B-b-but...''

With the pink on his cheeks turning to unsightly splotches, Will stomped to the desk and activated his computer.

Mac barked into the phone, telling Bud to get to publicity pronto.

Beside him Will fiddled with the computer a moment, then his face glowed pink again and a gasp flew from his taut lips. ''Well, this is just too much. They've deleted the promotional program from my work file.''

Mac dropped the phone into the cradle. ''What exactly is that?''

''*That—*'' disdain dripped from Will's voice ''—is the list of names and phone numbers of all my contacts in media land.''

Mac looked sick, as though the cereal he'd eaten was churning in his stomach. ''It's been deleted?''

''Like it never existed.'' Will tossed his head like an arrogant elf. Then he gave Mac a sly, wry grin. ''Oh, I forgot, *you* can't be expected to know anything about the running of this company. This department.''

Tia watched myriad emotions flash through Mac's eyes. Was Will toying with them? Or did he know Grant was dead? Know he was dealing with Mac?

"What does this mean to the launch?" Anger laced Mac's words.

"Total disaster." Will shrugged as though it meant nothing.

The heat drained from Tia's face and she knew she had to be as white as Holly Beary's fur. "No."

Will glanced at her then, spied her bandage and asked, "What happened to you?"

"I ran into a solid object," she said, wondering if Will had been the one who'd hit her.

He turned his limpid eyes back to Mac. "Really? Like to play rough, do you?"

Mac glared at him. "Did you make a hard copy of your contacts?"

Will smirked. "Remember yesterday when you asked me why I deserved a raise? I guess you'll see my worth now."

Mac glowered at Will, who didn't seem to realize he'd pushed the envelope to within inches of tearing it. "What the hell are you talking about?"

"Backup." Will's smirk turned to a wide grin. "I always back up my work on disks."

Mac's frown remained solid and Tia recalled that Grant backed up his work, too. But the backup disks had been stolen.

She hugged the envelope tighter. "Are you sure the backup disks aren't gone?"

"Would I mention them in that case?"

She wanted to rail at this infuriating man who kept answering questions with questions. Somehow she managed to keep her cool. Barely. "Why are you so sure they're here?"

"Because—" he patted his jacket pocket "—I al-

ways take them home with me. You don't think I'd
leave them here under the shifty eyes of that redheaded security idiot, do you?''

As though he'd heard himself being spoken about,
Bud Gibson walked into the office. ''Holy—''

He faced Mac with surprised eyes. ''What happened in here?''

''We were hoping you could shed some light on
that.'' Mac slumped, losing his Grant persona in his
dismay. Tia moved to his side, threaded her arm
through his and snuggled against him. She meant to
touch his spine covertly, but the simple act of linking
arms had him tensing, standing taller. Her pulse
skated erratically as their body connection sent fingers
of heat coursing through her.

Mac glanced at her a second, affection bold in his
gaze, the knowledge creating a war of joy and sorrow
in her heart. He returned his attention to the security
guard. ''When was the last time you checked this
floor?''

Bud wore a worried expression, as though he expected to be accused of vandalizing this office himself. ''A half hour before you arrived.''

''And the door was locked?'' Mac persisted.

''Yes, all the offices were.'' Bud shifted his gaze
from one to the other. Tia wondered if he was lying.
When his hazel eyes met hers, she glanced away. She
hadn't forgotten their confrontation and she wouldn't
court another.

But Bud wasn't about to ignore her. ''What happened T? Somebody conk you?''

She jerked back toward him, scowling. His eyebrows flickered. Was he the one who'd hit her? Or
was he as innocent as he seemed?

Mac said, "Did you hear any noises or anything, Gibson?"

Bud glanced at his boss and wiped his hands on his khaki pants. "No. Nothing out of the ordinary, so I didn't open any of the offices to look in. Guess maybe I'd better do that from here on out."

"Sounds like a plan, Stan," Will mumbled.

"A-are you calling in the cop—er, police?" Bud's face had gone ashen.

"No. But you can help Will clean this up. He has a busy day ahead of him." Mac covered Tia's hand with his, locking her to his side, and started for the door. A loving couple for all to see. "Oh, and, Will, make me a hard copy of your backup disk, would you?"

They strode down the hall. Mac held her close and Tia made no attempt to pull free. The morning had barely started and her stress level was higher than the Christmas tree in Rockefeller Center. Mac's touch had a more soothing effect than a dozen tranquilizers. A gallon of ice cream.

Too bad she couldn't enjoy it forever.

NANCY RICE'S DOOR stood open. She was inside, setting up for the day. She looked up as they passed. A frown flickered across her face and quickly disappeared as she batted her eyes at Mac. He pulled Tia closer, offered Nancy a quick hello, then they were inside his office. He shut the door behind them, releasing her with obvious reluctance.

A chill wafted over her as though he'd doused a fire she'd been sitting beside, stealing the warmth surrounding her. With a jolt Tia realized she was starting to care for this man too deeply, be affected by him with an intensity that could only bring her permanent heartache.

Mac said, "One disaster averted."

For a moment she thought he meant her. Then she realized he was talking about Will's problem. She ran her tongue across her dry lips. "Seems like the intruder at Grant's office was hedging his or her bet with this stunt."

Mac stared at her mouth a long moment. Desire tingled through Tia and thickened her throat. Mac took a step back, rubbing his jaw, seeming disconcerted, as well. "It was just something else to keep me from getting the toy shipped on schedule."

"We've been lucky so far." Tia found her voice and tapped the envelope. "Now we've got to figure out what Grant uncovered and see if we can't get one step ahead of our nemesis."

"Agreed." Mac glanced around the room as though seeing it for the first time, as though everything he knew had changed into something alien, as though he really was Grant and this was not the place he'd come to work every day for six long years. "I don't think, however, that we can start our investigation here."

"Where, then? Grant's condo?"

"No. Not my house, either. I don't know anything about surveillance work, but what if the killer tapped our phones?"

"How about my apartment?"

He thought a moment, then shook his head. "No. No good. It needs to be somewhere neutral. Someplace no one knows about."

She racked her brain. Who did she know who had

a place they could go and use the phones without worry? She thought of Molly Bowen. But she didn't want to go to the Bowens' and be sucked into celebrating the holidays with them. Couldn't face the slew of unhappy memories it would rouse. The worst thing was, she couldn't tell Molly the reason, couldn't tell anyone. Molly had tried to help her, done her the biggest favor in her life, but it had turned out all wrong—and ever since she'd learned the truth, she hadn't been able to look at Molly without recalling the horror.

"What's wrong?" Mac caught her chin and lifted it gently toward him as though he might kiss her. "You look like you've lost your best friend."

She started and pulled back, a nervous laugh spilling from her. "No. No, but I will if I don't call Ginny sometime this morning."

"Hey, maybe you could use her place?"

Tia's cheeks warmed. "Oh, not a good idea. She's Bud Gibson's sister, remember? What if he's involved in this?"

Mac blew out a frustrated breath. "There has to be someplace."

"Look, even if the phone is tapped, Grant's condo has a terrific security system. I can go there and start checking references right away this morning."

"What if the phone conversations are being taped?"

She shrugged. "So. I'll have a whole lot of information before anyone can get home to listen to the tapes. Our killer can't be in two places at once. He or she won't miss work—that would be totally suspicious."

"I don't want you doing this alone." Mac grasped

her hands, concern seeping through his strong, affectionate grip.

She forced her gaze from their locked hands, forced herself to meet his glance. "Why not?"

"It's not safe." Fear issued from him. "Look what happened to Grant."

"Grant wasn't killed at home." She swallowed hard, knowing she was splitting hairs. But she'd realized the danger they faced yesterday, realized there was no turning back—not if they wanted Grant's killer caught and the toy launched on time. She squeezed his hand. "I'm not particularly brave, Mac, but I couldn't live with myself if I didn't do whatever I could to see this thing through."

"Then we'll go to the condo and start in." He released her hands, his mind made up.

She caught him by the arm. "No. You've got to stay here. Keep an eye on your employees, keep the ball rolling toward Friday's shipment."

She could see he knew it. He didn't like it, but he knew it. "Okay. I'm probably going to have to ride herd on Will, anyway. Once I've made certain all departments are operating smoothly, I'll try and have that talk with Gwen."

She smiled. "Good luck."

He grew serious as he dug the car keys from his pocket. He reached for her hand, pressed the keys gently into her palm, then curled her fingers around them. He held her hand a full ten seconds, then traced a finger down her cheek, gazing at her as though memorizing her face. "Be careful."

KEEPING AN EYE on the rearview mirror, Tia drove to The Colliery restaurant in Renton. As far as she could tell, no one followed her from the plant. She parked, locking the envelope in the Porsche. Ginny's car was in the lot. She had likely already secured a booth and ordered coffee. Ginny always arrived first. It was an obsession, one of the few things she'd ever been able to control in her life.

Before she began making calls for Mac this afternoon, Tia wanted a few answers to her own mysteries. Answers only Ginny could provide.

The restaurant had made the usual concessions to the holiday—a gaily decorated tree, cards displayed behind the hostess station and carols playing softly in the background. The diners she passed were smiling at one another, exchanging gifts and happy tales.

Tia wondered what it would be like to feel joy at this most joyous time of year. She had no traditions to miss, no warm memories of happy Christmases past. Grant's murder had insured it would be a melancholy season forevermore.

She spotted Ginny, who was clutching a coffee mug as though trying to warm her hands. Apparently sensing her approach, Ginny glanced up at her, and her brown eyes lit up. Tia's pulse accelerated. This was the one person in the world she did consider family. Sister and friend. She slid into the booth opposite Ginny. The air was filled with the mouth-watering aromas of cooked food and steaming coffee from the cup before her. Her stomach gurgled and Tia realized she was hungry, despite the cereal she'd eaten at the condo earlier.

Ginny frowned at her. Touched her arm. "My God, what happened to your head?"

Tia fingered her bandage self-consciously, then waved her hand dismissively as though four stitches weren't holding her split flesh together. "Just a nasty encounter with a Christmas ornament. Long story better told on another day."

Uncharacteristically Ginny accepted that without question. Something was definitely amiss here. She seemed distracted. Her mind elsewhere. "How is Grant?"

Though Tia should have expected it, the question caught her off guard. Heat scrambled into her cheeks. How should she answer that? Honestly? In a public restaurant where someone might overhear? Fear flickered through her, and she glanced around, half expecting one of their suspects to be peering over her shoulder. Eavesdropping.

"Tia?" Ginny's expression held deep concern.

"Grant's doing as well as you'd expect—under the circumstances. He's...we're trying to get Mac's special Christmas toy shipped out as scheduled. It was important to Mac and G-Grant wants to see it through."

This news seemed to startle Ginny. "Then you've been to Coy Toys?"

"And seen Buddy, yes."

Ginny's face went so pale her freckles stood out. She heaved a shuddery sigh. "I know I should have told you weeks ago. But I didn't figure it mattered. I mean, Bud got the job on his own. All I knew at first was that he thought the world of his boss, Mac. How was I to know it was Mac Coy?"

Tia sipped her coffee. "When did you find out?"

"About a month ago." She seemed more nervous than ever.

About the time Tia had learned her awful secret.

''I was going to tell you, but I just never found the words. I'm such a coward.''

She covered her friend's hand with her own. Ginny had borne the onus of her three disreputable brothers most of her life. She wasn't the enemy here. She didn't deserve to be treated like one. ''Let's order something to eat.''

They gave their orders to the waitress, and when she was gone Ginny said, ''Bud swears he's reformed, Tia. I just don't know whether or not to believe him.''

Tia could see she wanted to, though. And she had the odd feeling Ginny wasn't telling all she knew. Tia recalled her own encounter with Buddy, the gun he'd wielded at Mac and her, and knew it would take more than Bud Gibson's word to convince her he'd reformed or was trying to change. But for Ginny's sake, she prayed her suspicions were wrong.

HALF AN HOUR LATER, with Ginny's borrowed laptop tucked on the car seat beside her, Tia headed for the condo.

Before she started making calls, she put a disk into Ginny's laptop and used her word-processing program to make a file for each of Mac's department heads. Then she began calling the people listed as references in each personnel record. As she verified the background of each employee, she added those notes to her files.

Already Mac had called her three times just to check on whether or not she was safe. Tia smiled. His calls were the only bright spot in this frustrating day. She hadn't uncovered one thing for Mac to be appalled about, to feel badly that he hadn't checked. So why had Grant left that message on her answering machine?

She set aside Will Holden's file and reached for Bijou Novak's. She'd been dialing and talking and typing notes into the computer for more than three hours. Her body was stiff from sitting too long. She stood and stretched, made a trek to the kitchen for a diet soda and returned to the living room.

The day was drifting toward evening, black shadows reaching across the landscape like a blanketing fog. Lights dotted the darkness across the lake. She closed the curtains and checked the security-alarm pad. The proper lights glowed reassuringly.

She settled down again and called the first reference Bijou Novak had listed. The phone number belonged to a department store that had done business in the same location for twenty years. Personnel had no record of anyone named Bijou Novak.

Tia tried another number with the same results. By the third call excitement swelled inside her like a fire of anticipation. She couldn't wait to talk to Mac.

As far as she could tell, before he'd hired her, Bijou Novak hadn't existed.

A violent chirping froze her fingers on the keyboard. Five seconds passed before she realized it was Grant's high-priced security system. The front door crashed open. Someone was in the condo with her.

Chapter Eleven

Mac's taxi pulled to a stop halfway into the parking area by Grant's condo. Fire trucks blocked further access. Alarm shot through him. He threw money at the cabby and jumped out. Smoke permeated the night air. He raced for Grant's condo, his heart pumping as hard as his legs.

His first sight of the condo turned his blood icy. The charred front door hung open like a pit into hell. Every instinct he had told him it was too late, but he ran for it, anyway. "Tia!"

A burly firefighter grabbed him. "Whoa, partner. You can't go in there."

Mac wrenched free. Started forward again. "Tia!"

The firefighter caught him again. "You live here?"

"Yes. What happened? Where's Tia?"

"Tia?"

"My fiancée!" Terror dried his throat. "She was here an hour ago!"

He started forward again, hauling along the burly man in heavy fire gear.

The firefighter said, "Look, buddy, an ambulance took a woman to Valley General about five minutes ago."

Mac stopped in his tracks. His heart fell to his toes, dragging his stomach with it. He began to shake. His mind conjured up all the horrors Tia might have suffered, from major burns to smoke inhalation. He rounded on the man. "Is...is she going to be okay?"

"I don't know." The guy shrugged.

Mac's control snapped. Fury and fear gripped him. He snatched hold of the man by the front of his coat and ground out through clenched teeth, "What *do* you know, man?"

The firefighter peeled free of Mac's grasp. "Looks like the Christmas tree caught fire. We should know for sure by tomorrow."

Mac felt stunned, shock beginning to numb his brain, his body. The Christmas tree? But the lights were those low-heat ones.

"Look, buddy, the condo isn't that bad." The firefighter shook his head. "We kept the fire from spreading beyond the living room. Of course, with smoke and water damage..."

"Water damage? From the sprinkler system?"

"No..." The man looked at him oddly, then began gathering hoses again. "Apparently that didn't activate."

Didn't activate? Mac stared at the man's back, his mind stumbling, his limbs frozen.

"Oh, my God, Grant." A middle-aged woman with bleached blond hair and thick glasses approached. "I'm so sorry. It was awful. Your burglar alarm went off—bleating like a lovesick ewe. I figured you'd hit the wrong button or something, but it went on and on and on."

The alarm? His eyes widened, but he could barely focus on the woman. Tia!

"I came over to see why you hadn't turned it off, and that's when I saw the smoke pouring out your open door."

The alarm? The sprinkler? The door was open? His fear for Tia tripled, stripping the lethargy from his body, his brain. Had someone broken in? "Did...did you see the young woman who was here?"

"Sorry." The neighbor shook her head. "Too much fire and smoke to see anything. I ran home and called 911."

"Was she hurt?"

"I don't know." The woman gave him a pitying look.

Mac shook himself. He had to get to the hospital. But how? He glanced around for his taxi. Gone. No! An acrid film coated his tongue: the taste of his own inadequacies. Grant would have known how to get to Tia. *He* never lost his cool in a crisis.

A bright spot of red glinted from the tangle of the fire trucks and hoses. The Porsche. Mac's pulse leaped. He dashed to the car and grasped the door handle. The alarm chirped at him. Damn. It was locked.

His scalp prickled as though it were shrinking on his skull. He considered smashing a window. But the car still wouldn't start without the key. Panic welled inside him. No. He had to think. Tia. Tia. Tia. He had to get to her. Where was that firefighter? Where was that neighbor? He gaze poked through the crowd. He couldn't find either of them. He spun left. Then right.

A soft jangle issued from his jacket. Keys. In his pocket. Hope hurried his hand to them. Mac held the key ring toward the street lamp.

"Yes!" he shouted, finding the spare car key.

Thanking God, he unlocked the car and jumped into the driver's seat. The powerful engine hummed at his touch. "I'm coming, Tia. Hang on, baby."

He tapped the gas. The car lurched forward. He pressed his foot down harder. The action energized him. Gave him the first sense of power he'd felt in days over his out-of-control life. He tore recklessly between fire engines, over fire hoses, past angry fire-fighters. He ignored them all, his only thought for the woman he loved.

The Porsche left the condo parking lot in a flash of speed.

Twenty minutes later he raced up to the information desk at Valley General Hospital. The elderly woman manning the station asked if she could help him.

He nodded, trying to catch his breath. "Tia Larken. She was brought in a while ago by ambulance."

"I don't have anyone by that name." She scanned her computer. "But if you're sure she was brought in by ambulance, perhaps she's in emergency."

"Of course." He should have thought of that. He ran for the stairs, flying down them two at a time. At the emergency counter, he again asked for Tia.

"I'm right here."

He jerked his head up at the sound of her voice. She was coming toward him. Walking on her own. Words failed him. He'd never seen a more beautiful sight. The horrible dread wrapping his heart began unraveling. He tripped toward her like a little boy on Christmas morning moving toward a favorite present.

As he walked Mac couldn't help taking inventory. No fire damage that he could see, no sign of smoke inhalation. Just some scratches on her cheeks. Nothing that looked like it wouldn't heal in a short time. Blowing out a relieved breath, he scooped her into his arms. Crushed her to him. Spun around with her, holding her close. Closer.

"I thought...I was afraid..." He put her down and leaned away. "Are you all right?"

"Other than a few scratches and some bruises," she assured him. But her face was abnormally pale and the smudges were back beneath her eyes. She'd suffered a terrible fright. Or worse.

Guilt flattened his relief. This was his fault. He'd gotten her into this. Insisted she get involved. "I'm so sorry."

She levered her hands against his chest and pushed away. "*You're* sorry? My God, *you* didn't break into the condo or set it on fire."

Horror spread through him. His worst fears were confirmed. "Someone broke in?" He leaned close, speaking low. "Then set fire to the condo? How did you escape?"

"I went over the balcony. Landed on some full but prickly shrubs," Tia whispered.

"Did you see who it was?"

"No. But we need to go somewhere and talk."

"Oh, yeah." He nodded and pulled her against his side, protecting her as best he could for the moment. But this wasn't enough. She had to get out of this sham. Had to stay as far away from it as possible. Even though the thought of facing the rest of the week without her left him cold, he had to send her away, before she suffered serious injury.

He would do that immediately after they talked.

MAC DROVE DOWN the familiar, narrow lane around Lake Kathleen, debating the wisdom of bringing Tia here. It was a mistake. He should have gone to her apartment. They could have talked there. Then he could have told her his decision to keep her out of this mess and left. What was the matter with him?

Fog swirled around the car in ghostly waves, adding to his distress. His neck prickled, and he tightened his grip on the steering wheel. He hadn't been here for a week. What if the killer had gotten in? Booby-trapped it somehow?

"Where are we?" Tia asked, peering out at the barn-shaped house looming out of the fog. A scattering of vapor lights, set on towering poles, shed an eerie glow over the property.

"Home, sweet home," he said with genuine warmth. He parked beside his old black Jaguar, which Bud Gibson had returned to the house the day Grant died.

He told Tia to wait a minute and hurried into the house.

Tia huddled in the Porsche, watching lights going on inside. She figured Mac was checking for intruders or signs of a break-in. After her experience earlier she appreciated his zeal. But the car was rapidly cooling, and the fog seemed to creep ever closer, perhaps hiding something or someone with evil intent.

She scrambled out of the car and up the porch, moving as quickly as her bruised body allowed. She slipped in the front door and closed it behind her, engaging the lock. Her breath came in short spurts and her pulse beat rapidly. She forced herself to take several slow breaths. To inspect her surroundings. She stood in a wide open foyer, with a staircase rising to her left and a solid rock wall directly ahead. She took

another, calmer breath and caught the scents of cold
fire ash, leather and wood polish.

Mac's house.

The thought warmed her insides as nothing had in
hours.

She heard the rustle of paper nearby and headed
across the plank flooring, past the rock wall and into
a great room. The kitchen ran the length of the house
to her right, a giant U-shaped, granite counter with
all black appliances, including the refrigerator.

As she stepped into his view, Mac glanced sharply
up, tension in every line of his body, until he realized
it was she. He stood at the fireplace, one knee on the
raised hearth, lighting the papers beneath a tepee of
kindling. "It shouldn't take too long to warm the
house."

He seemed disconcerted, as though uncomfortable
or shy at having her in his home.

"Thanks, but I didn't like being out there without…" She swallowed hard over the fact that she felt
a hundred times better just being near him. "Alone."

Self-conscious, she turned her attention to the
room. There was no sofa, just a pair of leather chairs
and ottomans facing each other near the rock fireplace. Beyond the fireplace built-in bookcases rose
above a wall-long counter that apparently served as
desk and work space. Strung along its surface were
phone, computer, fax, copier and other electronic
gadgets she couldn't identify.

The end wall seemed to be solid window, open to
the view, whatever that was. There were no curtains.
The glass glared their reflections back at her, but she
caught a dim image of some plants, overgrown and
intrusive, against the outside.

She glanced at Mac's reflection and saw he was looking at her with a sheepish grin. She spun around. He said, "There's a nice view of the lake from here...when I'm home in the daytime and think to trim the vegetation, that is. But I haven't had many daytime hours free lately. So right now the shrubs are encroaching on the house."

She smiled, glancing around again. Obviously picking up after himself wasn't one of Mac's priorities, either. And yet, for all its chaotic appearance, this house felt more like a home than Grant's spotless condo or her own pristine apartment.

Why? There was no symmetry of color or style, no common theme. The dining table was a picnic table with matching benches; the lamps consisted of a brass floor model, a high-tech desk fixture and a hanging wooden wagon wheel over the table; one leather chair was burgundy, the other navy blue. The hide had cracked at the arms and the headrests of both.

But like Mac, his house made no excuses for what it wasn't. What you saw was what you got. She wished she was as brave as he. But she doubted anyone had ever come into his home and turned it upside down, made it feel like one more place he wasn't safe.

She hugged herself.

"You still cold?" he asked. "You want some coffee?"

"No. I'd like something stronger."

"I've got some tequila." He nodded, understanding her request. "Or wine?"

"I think I could use the tequila, but I'll take the wine."

"How about something to eat?" He headed toward the kitchen.

She followed him, leaning on the counter as he opened the refrigerator. "What have you got?"

"I'd say our safest bet is a cheese omelet."

"You cook?"

He glanced over the refrigerator door and gave her a wry grin. "Most bachelors figure out one or two means of feeding themselves. I have a few specialties and I can use a microwave with the best of them."

He handed her the wine and corkscrew. "What happened at the condo?"

She told him about the break-in as she opened the wine. Her hand shook slightly, but she maneuvered the cork from the bottle and poured them both a glass. She took a sip of hers, then said, "I had just completed calling the references on Bijou Novak's job application when the alarm went off. For a second I didn't realize what it was. Then the door crashed open. Like I said, I didn't wait around to see who'd come calling. I just went out the glass door and dropped from the deck into the shrubs below."

Mac's face was ashen. "And this person, whoever it was, set fire to the condo?"

"Must have. Next thing I knew, smoke was pouring out of the open glass door. I ran to the next building and hid in the hedge until I heard the fire trucks coming."

Mac looked torn between sweeping her into his arms and smashing the wall. A cracking sound rent the thick tension separating them. Mac swore and looked at his hand. Egg was oozing through his fingers. Tia covered her mouth, barely holding in a laugh. "Do you always scramble eggs with your hands?"

Mac set the other eggs in the sink, then ran the tap. "It isn't funny. You might have been killed."

"But I wasn't, and I don't know about you—" she handed him a dish towel "—but I'm very grateful to be alive and able to laugh about something."

He dried his hands, then touched her chin. His gaze was tender and searching. "After tonight you're out of this sham. I won't have you in harm's way again."

Her dander flared at that. "You know what? I agreed to go along with you in order to help launch your toy. If in doing that we found Grant's killer, then so be it. But since last night, the person responsible has raised the stakes and made this even more personal than before. Burning the condo. Melting Ginny's laptop. Coming after me like that. No, I'm not *bowing* out. I'm going to help you *figure out* who's behind this."

"I don't want you hurt." He was adamant.

She lifted her chin defiantly. "Neither do I. So let's not waste time with ultimatums. We need to share information."

He looked ready to continue arguing. But she just shook her head at him. He picked up the eggs and began breaking them into the bowl. "Such as?"

"Such as—did you know that none of Bijou Novak's references panned out?" Tia set aside her wine and began grating cheddar into another bowl, working beside him, with him, anticipating his moves, as if they'd been doing this for years. "It's like she didn't exist before you hired her. She may have been the one at the condo this afternoon."

His brows twitched, then dove into a deep frown. "Couldn't have been Bijou. She was in my office just before I left."

"Darn." Tia sighed. "I suppose that would have been too easy. Do you know who might have been gone from the plant this afternoon?"

He poured the eggs into his omelet pan and poked at them with a spatula. "Will was at the printer's, Fred and Stewy followed a truckload of bears to the storage warehouse, and Suzanne had a dentist appointment."

"And Bud was off work." Tia handed him the cheese, then found dishes in one of the cupboards and set the picnic table. "Could have been any of them."

Mac grunted unhappily.

She concurred. This was getting them nowhere. How had Grant solved mysteries? She considered a moment and decided he probably used plain old logic—first checked the facts, found the inconsistencies in a suspect's stories and either proved them unimportant or the clue that solved the case. She and Mac were both intelligent people. They could figure this out. But where did they start?

With their list of suspects, of course. It occurred to her he hadn't mentioned his VP. "Did you have your talk with Gwen?"

He grimaced. "No. One of the techs called in sick, and she took his place in the lab working on the chips all day. So that'll have to wait until tomorrow."

Tia settled silverware next to the dishes, then paper towels for napkins. A thought struck her. "Are you sure Gwen was actually in the lab?"

"What?"

"Well...you know." She gestured with her hands. "All that protective gear required in the lab—how could you tell whether or not she was actually there? Did you speak with her?"

Mac's eyes widened. "No. Not in person. Just by phone. In the morning."

Tia pulled her hair behind her ear and tilted her head. "Great. The list keeps growing, instead of shrinking. What about Nancy?"

"Oh, Lord." He winced. "She was definitely at work."

And something, Tia realized, had definitely happened to cause him to look so embarrassed. Knowing Nancy, she guessed the woman had cornered him, caught him off guard somehow. An unexpected rush of jealousy and resentment sent heat into her cheeks. She bit back the urge to ask, hating that she reacted possessively about Mac. She had no right. Not to irritation or envy. This was none of her business.

If Mac wanted her to know details, he'd share them. Otherwise, she'd better stifle all curiosity. Maybe when this was ended—if Nancy proved not to be involved—maybe she and Mac... The thought left a bitter taste in Tia's mouth.

He carried the omelet pan to the table and spooned equal portions onto each plate. "She cornered me."

"She did?"

"Yes..." His voice trailed away as he sank onto the bench opposite her. He took a deep swallow of wine. "I can only think you're right—she must have seen Grant and Gwen together and assumes the engagement means nothing."

He spoke with a tenderness meant to protect her from the cruelty of the situation. But Tia knew nothing could protect her from the truth. She'd learned that the hard way. All you could do was deal with it. Somehow. "How did you handle it?"

He grinned, a self-deprecating lift of the corner of

his mouth. That bedeviling mouth. "In a most un-Grant-like manner. Let's face it, I don't have his... his...his anything."

He laughed at that. At himself. But she sensed deep down he might believe it, and she felt sad. He shouldn't compare himself to Grant. The differences were vast and wonderful. He lacked nothing. Tia touched his hand, riveting his gaze with hers. "Don't sell yourself short. Nancy would be lucky to have your love."

Any woman would.

He laughed at that. A tight, self-loathing bark. Tia wondered what she'd said wrong. Her concern must have shown on her face.

He said, "Grant would have handled the situation with more finesse."

Grant, Tia thought, would probably have taken Nancy up on her not-so-subtle sexual come-ons. Most healthy males would. She recalled her encounter with Mac the night before. He was definitely a healthy male. So why hadn't he given Nancy what she wanted?

Arguing with herself, she drank more wine, her courage building with every sip. Why not? Why not ask him? "Don't you find Nancy attractive, Mac?"

The question seemed to startle him. He laughed again. This time she couldn't identify his emotion from the tone. He reached for the wine bottle and refilled both their glasses. "Sure. I mean, what guy wouldn't?"

There was no conviction in his statement. His gaze met hers again and the heat in their turquoise depths was all for her. She tried looking away, but she seemed to be held in his glance, as mesmerized as the three wise men by the star in the east. She would follow him anywhere.

She blinked, the realization shocking her. She had no right to Mac. No right to encourage him. To keep him from pursuing a possible true love. Her heart pinched. She had to make him see that. To steer him in a better direction. Any direction away from herself. ''Why does Nancy make you so uncomfortable, then?''

Mac just stared at Tia, at her luscious lips, remembering the feel of that mouth beneath his. He forced his mind to Nancy, to the incident in his office, to her attempt to kiss him today. He'd backed away from her like a man running from terrorists. Nancy's lips weren't haunting his dreams. Tia's were. He wanted her so badly he could think of little else, could barely keep his mind on the launch.

''Why, Mac?''

She was staring at him with those damn, distracting emerald eyes, and by God, at this moment, with two glasses of wine bolstering his confidence, he decided to share his secret with her. ''It isn't Nancy—''

It's you. But he bit off the words before he embarrassed her as much or more than he'd embarrass himself. Why had he even considered telling her this?

''Then what is it, Mac?''

''It's me,'' he blurted. ''I...I haven't had...er, any experience with the fair sex.''

Tia lifted her eyebrows. Whatever she'd expected him to say, it wasn't this. Disbelief reached into every corner of her mind. She shook her head. She'd been held by this man. Tenderly. Sexily. Her gaze fell to his generous mouth. Her pulse quickened. She'd been kissed by him in ways that fired her blood and haunted her imagination. His claims were false. "I don't believe you."

His expression was serious. Earnest. "I'm not Grant. My life has been computers and electronics. My lab. My toys. Kids. Women—" the tips of his ears were bright red "—make me too...nervous."

Too nervous? What exactly did that mean? Tia was taken aback...and touched. Mac's shyness endeared him to her more than she expected. She hadn't noticed he was too nervous. He was staring at her lips again. Her blood began to simmer. Her gaze lowered to his mouth, and all the sweet memories of his kisses came to haunt her, to tease her with need.

As though he'd read her like a book, Mac moved to her bench and pulled her into his arms. All her intentions of letting him go, of pushing him away were lost in a power she didn't understand and couldn't fight.

His kiss, at first timid, quickly grew bold, demanding, and robbed her resistance, rousing such need through her, it pulled her down into a whirlpool of swirling passion. For a man without experience, he knew instinctively all the ways to leave her breathless. Her whole body, her entire mind, burned for want of him; it was like nothing she'd ever felt.

Mac pulled back. His eyes were so glazed, his manner so rattled, Tia realized he hadn't exaggerated his lack of finesse with the ladies. He might not be a virgin, but he wasn't Don Juan, either. A strange feeling filled her heart, a deepening of her affection for this man.

Somehow his innocence made him even more appealing. Just as kissing and encouraging him was even more dangerous. She had to stop this now. She opened her mouth to speak. Mac's lips claimed hers with renewed fervor. She placed her hands on his chest. She would push him away. She would. His tongue danced with hers. And every promise she'd just made herself dissolved in the magic that was Mac Coy.

Chapter Twelve

Mac could no more stop kissing Tia than he could stop breathing. But he knew he should. Even as her sweet soft mouth invited him inside, he knew it. Even as her bedeviling tongue stroked his—promising delights without end—he knew it. Even as her delicate hands pressed against his chest like conduits flowing with love, he knew it.

He skimmed his fingers over her back, exploring, learning, memorizing the planes and curves of her. His blood thickened, heated, his need swelling hard and tight. The air seemed to be sucked from his lungs in tiny spurts. His heart thrummed against her palms. Her skin yielded to his touch.

With every ounce of his being he ached to give himself over to her completely, to trust her with his feelings, his hopes, his dreams. His secrets.

And yet how could he? Yes, he loved this woman—but she loved his brother. Still, she was responding to him, sighing at his touch, urging him on. She wanted him, too. Or did she? An awful thought cooled his fevered brain. Was she kissing him like this from her desire to hang on to all that remained of Grant? Because he looked like Grant? Reminded her of Grant? Cold washed his veins, drained his ardor. As sad as the possibility made Mac, he couldn't blame her if she was.

But he didn't want her that way.

He pulled back, his chest heaving, his heart thudding like a shutter in the wind. "This...this isn't—"

"No," Tia said breathlessly. "Don't..." *Don't explain. Don't apologize.* Her cheeks burned with guilt. Shame. She shouldn't have let it go this far. Shouldn't have encouraged him. Shouldn't have taken advantage of his hunger to be with a woman. Any woman.

The awful guilt she saw in his eyes proved she was right. Despite his knowledge of Gwen and Grant, she, Tia, still wore his brother's ring. Mac still thought of her as the woman grieving for his brother. If she allowed him to make love to her, afterward he might never forgive himself.

No matter that it was Mac she wanted. Not Grant. The fact remained that he deserved a woman who could promise him a future. That woman was not Tia Larken. She felt her heart cracking, a long jagged pain cutting across her chest. There were too few men like Mac Coy in this world. Whomever he fell in love with would be one lucky woman. Tia just wasn't sure she could stand that woman being Nancy Rice.

Mac grabbed their empty plates and headed into the kitchen. He'd be damned if he'd apologize for kissing her, for wanting her. Yes, it was wrong. He shouldn't have taken advantage of her vulnerability, but he wasn't going to lie about it, to her or to himself. He yanked open the dishwasher and plunked the plates into it, then began cleaning the bowls and omelet pan.

When he finished, he straightened and glanced

around for Tia. She stood near the fireplace gazing into the flames, looking careworn and in need of protection. He yearned to rush to her, to pull her into his arms again. But he feared where that would lead. He cursed under his breath. Why couldn't it be Tia, instead of Nancy, who wanted him? Who...

His mind tripped loose a memory. What was it Nancy had said to him just before he'd left today? The office Christmas party. In all the excitement at Grant's condo, he'd forgotten it again.

He groaned and Tia spun toward him. "What?"

"Weeks ago I turned the company party over to Bijou to handle." He hung the dish towel on the refrigerator-door handle and started toward Tia. "It's tomorrow night at the Wilderness Golf and Country Club. Henry's Switch Bar and Grill is catering."

"A party?" She looked dismayed. "Under the circumstances shouldn't it be canceled?"

He nodded sheepishly. "Normally losing the CEO would be reason to call off a company party."

"But?" Her brows twisted with disbelief.

"But 'Mac' wouldn't want the party canceled because he'd had the misfortune of meeting an untimely and accidental demise."

"And?"

"And I think it would be wise not to let the killer know that we suspect foul play in my brother's death." He shoved his hand through his short hair. "Plus, I'd like the opportunity to observe everyone without the cloak of work around them. Maybe he or she will let down their guard."

She considered a moment. "I guess it might be interesting and maybe even informative to observe our suspects interacting in a social setting."

"Of course this year won't be the all-night bash I usually throw—and we only need to put in an appearance."

She glanced at the fire again, then back at Mac. "I take it you normally love Christmas?"

Mac moved to the navy leather chair and settled into its comfortable, familiar cushions. He gazed up at Tia. "As far back as I can remember this has been my favorite holiday."

"And my least favorite." Her emerald eyes darkened to forest. She hugged herself as though the heat from the burning logs offered no warmth.

Anger flared inside Mac. Grant's death had insured that Tia would forever deplore this time of year. His heart ached for her. For them both. But he, at least, had happy memories to call up when morose ones threatened.

She took the chair across from him.

Mac leaned toward her, placing his forearms on his thighs. "I liked everything about Christmas—playing a shepherd in the Sunday-school pageant, the anticipation Grant and I shared about opening presents, the huge meals prepared by our mom and Grandma Coy, and in recent years, my participation with the children at the shelters." He flung an arm outward. "Usually I have this place decked out like a department store. But then, I don't usually have a Christmas-toy shipping three weeks before the twenty-fifth. Holiday merchandise goes out in October at the latest. This is usually our slow time."

Her head was tilted to one side. She was listening, but seemed to be waiting for the other shoe to drop. "And now?"

His heart felt as heavy as a sleigh full of presents

with no destination. "Grant's murder will always color the season with sadness, but as long as I create toys, as long as children believe in Santa, I'll feel like I'm a part of Christmas."

She tucked her hair behind her ear. "Then why did you groan just now?"

He blew out a noisy breath. "Because I won't be going to the Christmas party as Mac." He pointed at his suit. "I can wear this again tomorrow, but not again tomorrow night. And it's the last of Grant's clothes in my possession."

She put her hand over her mouth. "Oh, dear. The fire."

He nodded, thinking he'd prefer his own clothes. He supposed, however, that was out of the question.

"Clothes are the least of our worries." She touched his knee. "I'll call Nordstrom's in the morning. They have Grant's sizes and his personal tastes on file."

"Of course, I hadn't realized—" He broke off, a knife of jealousy stabbing his heart. How could he hope to win her heart—her mind—when both were so full of Grant? "I guess all we need now is to figure out who killed Grant and how we can prove it."

FIRST THING NEXT MORNING they collected the phone records for the year from Nancy and took them into Mac's office. They sat on opposite sides of the worktable with pages spread between them. Tia asked, "What are we looking for?"

He glanced over at her, his expression so like Grant's it caused her heart to trip with pain. And worry. Was Mac becoming more like Grant, or was it just her imagination? No, it *was* her imagination.

And her fear he'd lose the qualities that made him uniquely Mac.

The confusion in his eyes told her that. Grant would have attacked these phone records with purpose, his course of action honed from years of experience. Mac was as much at sea as she was.

He shrugged and suggested, "Calls to Taiwan?"

The phone company separated the calls according to long distance and international, listing each call beneath the extension it originated from. Each department head had his or her own four-digit extension. So tracking who called where was fairly easy, if complex. Coy Toys, Tia realized, liked reaching out and touching others around the world.

The interoffice phone rang. Mac crossed to his desk and answered it. "Yes?"

Tia watched his expression darken, then fill with alarm. "I'll be right there."

He hung up and started for the door at a clip. "That was Gwen. She says there's a problem in the lab."

Tia's stomach grabbed. "Sabotage?"

"No, she says it's minor. I hope to God she's right. If I can't correct it straight away, it will slow down production."

"Mac, wait!" An awful thought struck her. "Why would Gwen call Grant to fix something in the lab?"

Mac stopped, his hand on the doorknob, confusion tweaking his eyebrows. "What?"

Just the thought of that woman—no, *any* woman— touching Mac, kissing Mac, sent acid burning through her belly. She grappled with her jealousy, reminding herself Mac was not hers. His romantic encounters, solicited or not, were none of her business. But she couldn't allow his fear for the launch to trip them up.

To give them away. "Gwen wouldn't call Grant for an emergency in the lab. He was a detective, not an electronic whiz. It's more likely she wants to see 'you' alone."

He laughed at the irony, slapping his forehead. "Oh, damn. You're right. And I almost went bursting down there intent on repairing the 'problem.'"

The realization of what actually faced him in the lab sent dread flashing through his eyes. But it was nothing as sharp as the alarm of a moment ago. He rubbed his jaw and glanced at the phone as though reconsidering Gwen's end of the conversation. This time without the panic he'd felt the first time.

He straightened his tie, his cuffs, then his jacket. He squared his shoulders and gave Tia a small grin. At the moment he looked exactly like Grant. "If I'm not back in an hour, send help."

"Good luck." Tia forced her own smile. Gwen could do a lot of sensual convincing in an hour. The images in her head fed the jealousy she'd tried denying. "I'll keep at these while you're gone."

Making herself concentrate on the work at hand, Tia started with January, methodically scanning each month's billing. In July she found the first call to Taiwan. She frowned. Was this Lei Industries' number? Or did it belong to another company in Taiwan? For all she knew, Mac used lots of "made in Taiwan" parts for his toys. But then, wouldn't the Taiwan numbers have shown up earlier in the year? There was one way to find out. She reached for the phone and dialed. A couple of minutes later her suspicion was confirmed.

She replaced the receiver with a trembling hand and boiling ire. What nerve using Mac's own phone to sell him out! She'd known their nemesis had guts, but this struck her as rubbing Mac's nose in it. Why? Was the betrayal personal? Was someone getting even while getting rich?

She jotted the number on her notepad, and continued going through the phone records, noting the dates and length of the calls each time she found the same number. There were several more, right up to this month's billing.

Tia leaned back in her chair. Unless she was mistaken, they all seemed to have been made from the same extension. The one in Bijou Novak's office. She tapped her pencil on the pad. The calls to Taiwan weren't all she found interesting. There were also a lack of calls to Mexico and a slew of calls from Suzanne's line to one area of Seattle. What the hell was going on?

She needed to hash this out with Mac. She glanced at her watch. He'd been gone twenty minutes. What was taking so long? Was there a real problem, something that could shut down or slow down production? If so, Bud Gibson would have some mighty big explaining to do.

More likely, though, Gwen was plying her case with "Grant." Unwanted images filled Tia's head. Gwen's hands on Mac, her body pressed to his, his body reacting as it had to her, Tia. The urge to rush down there and burst in on them grabbed her. She began pacing, her gaze flying about the room as she walked.

All the glittery decorations seemed to mock her, remind her of a childhood she could not overcome. She spotted Holly Beary on the shelf. She crossed to the toy and reached for it. The plush fur felt silken against her fingertips. She touched the heart-shaped chip, awed by the magic knowledge it possessed, the technology Mac had discovered from his desire to make the lives of lonely children less so.

She caressed the holly berries at the toy's neck. She would have loved having a teddy bear like this when she was little. A friend to pour her heart out to, to hug and hold on those scary nights when it seemed no one wanted her. When her heart ached with such emptiness, she would often throw up.

The ugly memories swelled inside her mind like a dark cloud, a living, breathing entity that could and would possess her, that knew the truth about her, that knew just how unworthy she was. Her palms dampened. She didn't deserve a toy as fine as this. She pushed the bear away and stumbled back.

She circled the worktable once more. The room seemed to be closing in on her. Where was Mac? Another half hour had passed. She didn't dare go to the lab, but she couldn't stay here a minute longer. She decided to talk to Bijou.

She rode the elevator to the second floor. As she stepped into the hall, she faced the lab. The door was closed, the blinds drawn. For privacy? For a tryst? Her mouth went dry and Tia stamped down the unwelcome images springing into her mind. She would not burst in on them and embarrass Mac.

A nerve ticked against her temple. She moved past the lab and down the hall. The sales department was the last office on the left. Voices filtered from the room in between. She hadn't noticed yesterday, but now realized this was the employee lunchroom. There were no blinds on these windows. Several people sat at a round table enjoying their morning break. Bijou was among them, her back to Tia.

Tia stopped, uncertain whether or not to enter the lunchroom. But no one glanced at her. Just as well, she decided. She'd wait for Bijou in her office. Best speak to her in private.

But as she approached the sales office, Tia noticed the door stood ajar. Someone was inside speaking. She nudged the door open and peered in. Suzanne sat at Bijou's desk, the phone to her ear. She glanced sharply up at Tia. Her dark eyes widened. She mumbled into the phone and hung up. She stood, smoothed her sleek cap of short black hair and walked toward Tia. "Bijou is next door. Did you need something?"

Guilt telescoped from her.

Tia shut the door with her heel and leaned against it. "I wouldn't mind having a minute of *your* time if you could spare it, Ms. Chang?"

"Of course." She twisted her hands together. "And please, call me Suzanne."

Tia nodded. She had the feeling she was holding a tiger at bay with nothing to protect herself but the air that separated them. The sensation was crazy. She had six inches and ten pounds on Suzanne. "Grant and I were just going over the telephone records and I found the most curious thing."

"Really?" Suzanne's brows lifted slightly.

"Yes." Tia deliberately kept her voice soft. "Did you know there wasn't one phone call to Mexico? Not one in the whole year."

Twin dots of color sprang to Suzanne's cheeks, and Tia could almost hear her brain scrambling. But she said nothing.

Tia prodded, "If no calls were made to Mexico, how can you be in touch with the factory?"

Tia clenched her fists, waiting for the head of product marketing to speak. Someone was making the teddy bears. But who? Someone in Taiwan? Her breath hitched at the possibility. Was Suzanne behind all this? Had she lied about the plant in Mexico? Killed Grant when he found out? Broken into Grant's office and then his condo?

Could this tiny woman have hit her with the silver star?

She reassessed her judgment of Suzanne's size and strengths. Being tiny wouldn't have deterred the person who'd betrayed Mac. Who'd murdered Grant. Was Suzanne that person? Did she have a motive, a need for instant riches Mac knew nothing about? "Is there even a factory *in* Mexico?"

"Are you addled?" Suzanne made a face as though she thought Tia had lost her mind. "Of course there's a factory. It's in Juarez. Across from El Paso. We...we converse via e-mail. *That* is a local call, for your information."

Tia tensed. Did that explain the slew of local calls? She didn't own a computer. Knew zip about getting or sending e-mail. But even if Suzanne's explanation was the truth, surely there would be one or two long-distance phone calls. Or faxes. She couldn't believe e-mail was the only way they conversed.

"I really need to get back to work." Suzanne's tone was impatient, and Tia realized she was still guarding the door.

She stepped aside and Suzanne darted out. Tia stared after her, unconvinced that she'd learned the whole truth. Suzanne was too nervous. But what she believed and what she could prove were not one and the same. Grant would have known the right questions to ask Suzanne. But she, Tia, wasn't Grant— any more than Mac was. She mulled over what she'd been told. Were the local calls to the one area in Seattle made to access the Internet?

Tia strode across the room to the window. The morning was as gloomy as her thoughts, both decidedly in sharp contrast with this office decor. Like most of the others, Bijou had given in to the holiday spirit, but here all the decorations were handmade. By a child. She leaned against the wall, studying the adornments on the tree more carefully. Curiosity wound through her. What child had made these paper bells and stars? What little hand had pasted on the sparkles? Bijou's own child?

The thought roused a wealth of conflicting feelings in Tia. Could a mother who loved a child this much be a murderer?

The office door opened. Tia tensed, frozen in place. The person entering didn't see her, but headed straight for Bijou's desk, dropped into her chair and grabbed the phone.

Like yesterday he was dressed for work in the warehouse. He began punching numbers on the phone, enough for Tia to realize he was not making a local call. She stepped toward him. "Who are you calling, Stewy?"

He dropped the receiver as though she'd shot it from his hand. "Holy—" His Adam's apple bobbed, setting his dreadlocks into similar bouncing mode. "Whoa. You tryin' to give a dude a heart attack?"

"No. I was standing next to the tree. I guess you

didn't see me.'' Tia blew out a breath, her muscles easing. ''I'm waiting for Bijou.''

''She's next door.'' Stewy pointed. ''In the lunch-room.''

Tia nodded. ''Does she know you're using her phone?''

''Sure.'' He shrugged, looking as though he'd like to ask where Tia got off questioning him about this. But he seemed to think better of being insolent. She held the same leverage over all the employees—except perhaps Gwen. They couldn't be sure what her status in this company was yet. How it might affect their future with Coy Toys.

''I don't know.'' Stewy levered up out of the chair as though he weighed a ton. ''She don't mind, though. Everybody does it. 'Cause, you know, it's convenient.''

''Oh.'' For the second time in the past few minutes Tia's belief that Bijou was a murderer rent like paper through a shredder. Any of Mac's employees might have come into this office when Bijou was away from her desk. Any of them could have used her phone for the calls to Lei Industries. But why had she lied on her employment application? Why hadn't she existed until Mac hired her?

Frustration tightened Tia's nerves. Hell, maybe Bijou *had* made the calls. Tia glanced at the decorations again. Maybe she needed the money for the child in her life.

Fred poked his head through the doorway. ''You done, Stewy?''

''Yeah. I'm coming, dude.''

''Well, shake a leg. We're about ready to haul the morning's load to the warehouse.'' He spotted Tia and his froggy eyes lit up with a lustful glint that made her skin crawl. As usual he gnawed the butt end of a wooden matchstick. He kept staring at Tia, undressing her with his gaze. "See you at the party tonight."

Tia shuddered inwardly.

"Seems like you're having a party in here." Bijou entered, toying with one of the pencils that poked from her French roll. She glanced from one to the other as though awaiting an explanation for the crowd gathered in her office.

Fred and Stewy bade her goodbye and left.

Ignoring Tia until she was settled behind her desk, Bijou seemed nervous. But when she glanced up, her aqua eyes held only curiosity. "If Mr. Coy sent you, please assure him everything is going full steam ahead on my end."

Tia gave the room another cursory glance. "I didn't realize you had a child."

Bijou stiffened. "It's not a crime, last I looked."

Tia studied Bijou. Why would she suggest having a child was illegal? "I didn't say it was."

"No, of course not." She blushed, then looked flustered. "Is there something in particular I can do for you?"

Tia wanted more information about this woman's child, about Bijou in general, but if Bijou was the killer, asking her directly might be dangerous. She decided to hold her questions for another time. When Bijou's guard might be down. Say, tonight at the party. Maybe after a couple of drinks Bijou would be more willing to open up to a sympathetic ear. "I...I heard you were in charge of the company party. I just wondered if there was anything you needed help with.''

''No. It's handled.'' She gave Tia a smile of appreciation. ''But thanks for asking.''

''Well, then, we'll see you tonight.''

Not wanting to pass the lab, Tia took the stairs to the third floor and hurried back to Mac's office, more anxious to see him than ever. To her relief he was there. He looked awful. Like the loser in a war.

The acid in her stomach doubled. ''Was the problem mechanical?''

He shook his head. ''No. You were right.''

She spotted a smear of lipstick on his crisp collar, and her throat constricted. She wanted to rush to him, to brush it away, as she couldn't brush away the pictures filling her head, twisting her heart. ''Are you... okay?''

''Better than Gwen.'' His eyes glazed over like a soldier looking inward, seeing some internal horror. ''She's not too pleased about 'my' refusal to break up with you until after the toy is launched. She threatened and cajoled and—''

He broke off, the tips of his ears pink. ''I'm not sure if she believes my lie.'' He ran his hand through his hair. ''You'd think by now I'd be getting better at it. It feels like my whole life is one big fabrication.''

Tia bit back the sympathetic smile that sprang to her lips. ''I don't think it's an art you want to develop.''

He lifted an eyebrow at her. The warmth issuing from his eyes reached inside her and chased the chill from every corner of her being. She felt her blood heating. Felt the dangerous sizzle of attraction that existed between them sparking with new life.

His eyes darkened. Did he feel it, too? "Where were you?"

She ran her tongue across her lips, stemming the tide of unbidden feelings his very glance aroused. She explained her findings among the phone records and what she'd discovered on the second floor.

He blew out a huge breath. "Well, this is getting us nowhere fast."

"Maybe you should question Suzanne. I swear she was as nervous as a cat about something. Her face went bright red when I told her there were no phone calls to Mexico. Something isn't right about that, Mac."

The fine lines of worry around his eyes deepened. His wonderful mouth tensed. The stress of this launch weighed heavy on him. And Tia feared the deceptions ran deeper than either of them suspected.

"Come on, then." Mac gestured for her to join him. "I want to talk to Fred about that warehouse shipment, anyway."

Before they reached the door, the interoffice phone rang. Mac hurried to it. "Yeah?"

His face drained of all color. He cursed.

Tia lurched toward him, her stomach dropping like an axed tree. "What—?"

He waved her off, disconnected the caller, then immediately poked a series of buttons on the phone. A second later his voice rang through the intercom system. "Everybody. There's a fire on the first floor. This is not a drill! Stay calm and get out of the building! Now!"

He dialed 911. Shouted for a fire truck, then grabbed Tia and herded her into the hall.

Chapter Thirteen

"Mac, wait!" Tia wrenched from his grasp. Her eyes were wild with shock. "The phone records—we might need them."

He frowned, reaching for her again. Anxiety clawed his gut. They were running out of time. "I thought you had them."

"No." She started back toward the office door. "I left them on the worktable."

"Well, they weren't there when I returned." He caught her hand and pulled insistently. "Forget them. We need to leave. Now."

"Yes, of course." She shook her head as though trying to clear it. She quit fighting him.

But he could still see panic in her eyes.

She gulped as though choking. "You said the fire is on the first floor. How bad is it?"

"I don't know." Stewy hadn't said. There hadn't been time. "I'll worry about that once everyone's safely outside."

They hurried past Nancy's office. The door stood wide open. Mac glanced in, relieved to see no one was inside. Will's studio was also vacated. The new artwork stood vulnerable to this latest attack by

Grant's killer. It hadn't been ready to mail yesterday. Would it be destroyed by the fire raging on the first floor? As the morning's output of bears was now being destroyed?

His body flushed, but Mac shoved the thought away and rushed Tia into the stairwell. It reverberated with the slap of descending footfalls and anxious voices, but was fortunately free of smoke.

A woman's sobs skipped up to them. Below, Mac spotted Nancy and Will. Nancy was stumbling down the steps as though her legs were made of rubber. Will struggled to keep her erect, moving, clasping her arm and urging her forward. He was stronger than he appeared. His high-pitched voice cut through her terrified wails. "Nan, could you step it up?"

Mac and Tia took Will's advice, clambering down the steps, quickly catching up to them. The second-floor crew jammed the stairwell ahead. All six were still dressed in the sterile lab suits. Clutching Tia's hand tightly, Mac hauled her past Will and Nancy. He craned his neck, searching over the tops of the lab workers, seeking Gwen. The staircase curved, making it impossible to see to the bottom landing.

Tia felt as though she were being tugged along like a toddler's pull toy. With every downward step, her terror escalated. Her mind screamed for her to run. But her legs felt leaden, uncontrolled by her brain. Was the fire just beyond the last door? Would they be trapped, forced to retreat to the higher floors? She'd never wanted out of a building more than she wanted out of this one now. If she could climb over the crush of bodies between Mac and the exit, she would.

The realization shamed her. Shocked her back from

the edge of hysteria. *Calm down,* she chanted to herself. But despite her best effort, her pulse careered out of control, and her hand was slick inside Mac's. She'd escaped being burned to death last night. She might not be that lucky today.

As though he'd read her thoughts, Mac gave her hand a squeeze. And she thanked God he was here with her. At least she wasn't facing this alone.

"Gwen!" Mac shouted over the heads of lab workers.

"I'm here, Grant!" They couldn't see her, but the tenderness in her voice rang through the crowded stairwell. She sounded as though she'd forgive "Grant" in a heartbeat. Despite the terror of the situation, Tia felt a pang of jealousy.

He answered, "Are you sure there's no one left on the second floor?"

"I have all my people and no one was in the lunchroom!"

The lab workers moved farther down the steps.

"Bijou?" Mac asked, pushing closer to the exit.

"I didn't see her!" Gwen hollered. "Her office was empty!"

"She said something about cutting out early to attend to some last-minute details for the party tonight," Will said.

Nancy's pretty face was streaked with mascara and her eyes were too wide. She'd stopped sobbing, but was trembling so hard Will's golden hair shivered.

"Grant!" Gwen shouted again. But Mac could see her now as the dozen of them jammed near the bottom landing. Her normally pale cheeks were flushed with anxiety. Her keen blue eyes behind the glasses were narrowed in fear. "Smoke's seeping in beneath this door."

Gasps ran through the crowd, and Nancy wept anew.

Terror raked cold fingers of fear through Mac. "Don't open it!"

"Well, we can't just stand here." She spun toward the door, reached out and gingerly felt it. "The surface is cold. The knob is cold. I'm going to open it."

Everyone seemed to suck in air at once. The silence in the stairwell was thick enough to slice. Tia heard the roar of her pulse in her ears. But above it, the click of the disengaging door mechanisms sounded like a rifle shot. Gwen swung the door open.

Ugly black smoke raced inside, setting off the detectors in the ceiling overhead. Over the nerve-jarring bleats, Mac hollered, "Get down, everyone! On your knees. And turn to the right the second you're over the threshold and follow the wall to the outside door!"

As quickly as space allowed, people fell to all fours and began crawling with the speed of a centipede. Tia felt Mac behind her, but feared she'd lose him in the dense smoke. She could see nothing. Could only hear people coughing. She felt as though she were being sucked forward like snow sliding off a sun-warmed cabin roof.

Why weren't they going faster? The acrid stench stung her nostrils. And no matter how low she ducked her head, she couldn't elude the stinging mist that bit at her eyes. She held her breath. Her lungs burned, pleading for one gulp of fresh oxygen. But she didn't exhale or inhale until they were outside in the crisp December air.

Then she gulped in several deep breaths. Nothing had ever tasted so sweet. Or felt so delicious. Except for Mac's arms snaking around her now, pulling her tight and snug into the safe harbor of his embrace. Except his whispered, "We made it, love."

She hugged him back, melting in the security and contentment that being held by Mac gave her. She wanted to shout with joy, but was too overcome. Her nerves shivered, then steadied. She was alive. Mac was alive. Life was far from perfect, yet at that moment nothing seem insurmountable.

But reality shattered the moment as their awareness of others intruded. Several people were coughing, wiping at their eyes, moving rapidly away from the building. White lab suits were soot-streaked. Tainted. The smoke rolling from the building was quickly turning the sweet air acrid. Bitter.

Mac seemed not to notice. He had released her and was counting heads, making sure his employees had made it out alive. People first. Things later. Tia's heart swelled with love. How could twins, so alike on many levels, grow up to have such opposite values? With Grant, it was things first, people second. Mac held his brother in high esteem, but Grant couldn't touch Mac in a single way that counted with her. Grant was the one who couldn't fill his brother's shoes.

In the distance she heard the unmistakable shriek of fire engines and ambulances approaching. The sound galvanized Mac. He took off, running around the building to the shipping docks. Tia followed, then hung back. Smoke was rolling from the open bays. Suzanne Chang and her staff, along with the daytime security guard, milled outside, watching in horror.

Only Stewy seemed to be trying to put the fire out. In the midst of the blaze, he was spraying frantically with a large fire extinguisher. Mac scrambled up the steps and into an open dock, found another extinguisher and began helping.

Within seconds the firefighters arrived. They ordered Stewy and Mac outside and soon had the fire out. Paramedics worked diligently, checking Coy Toys employees for smoke inhalation, treating them for irritated eyes, treating the minor burn Stewy had gotten on his leg in his efforts to douse the flames.

Mac stood to one side, looking stricken, as though his whole world were a burned-out, watered-down mess like the pile of ruined boxes. Tia's heart ached for him. The day's output of bears would be as sooty as Santa's boots. Even if they could get back into production by morning, they'd lost product and time.

This was a staggering blow to the launch. The point of sending the whole shipment out on Friday was that it would arrive in stores across the country this weekend and be put on sale everywhere by the following Wednesday, the date promised in all the campaign ads.

It hadn't cost them the launch, but it meant making adjustments in the shipments. It meant angering longtime customers. Blackening Mac's hard-earned reputation. She supposed his customers would understand, under the circumstances. But that wouldn't make Mac feel any better. She edged closer to him and slipped her arm through his.

He curled his hand over hers, his mouth easing as he gazed down at her. But there was such incredible pain in his eyes.

"Don't look so worried, boss man," Stewy said. "It was only the empty boxes that burned."

Mac nodded, knowing he should be grateful. Tia was with him. Safe and sound. None of his employees had suffered serious injury. The fire chief had just assured him there was no structural damage to the building; the fire *had* been contained to the boxes.

A slight breeze blew through the open bays, chasing out the lingering wisps of smoke. As soon as the fumes lessened, it would be safe to go back inside. A cleaning crew could make short work of the soot.

All this should have cheered him, but he felt defeated. Frustrated. Anger, that alien emotion, churned like a tornado inside him. "I know, Stewy, but this morning's output of bears is lost."

"Yeah." Stewy sighed, shaking his head wearily, his gaze on his wounded leg. A second later he jerked his head up as though he'd been slapped. His eyes were wide and he pointed to the parking lot. "No. No, they're not, dude. We got both trucks loaded for the warehouse. All the bears are out there. The new arrivals won't be here until this afternoon."

Mac gaped at Stewy. What had he said? The bears were not in the building? He struggled to pull in a breath. His lungs resisted. He felt more stunned than ever at this stroke of good luck. "Are you saying…nothing was actually damaged?"

"That's right. Might have been if Fred and I had already left for the warehouse and the fire'd gone undetected. But Fred told me to wait in the truck while he saw a man about a horse, you know?" Stewy glanced at Tia and looked embarrassed. "He was gone forever. So I came looking to see if he'd keeled over in the john. Dude eats way too many Twinkies.

Anyway, that's when I noticed there was smoke everywhere. I buzzed the security guy. He bopped after the Chang gang. Hustled 'em the hell out of there. I called you and started with the extinguisher.''

The fire trucks pulled out of the parking lot. Mac glanced around. The Medic One van stood to one side. A woman in a blue uniform was speaking to one of ''the Chang gang.'' But not Fred. He tightened his grip on Tia and glanced at Suzanne, found the guard and Gwen and Will and Nancy. A frown twisted his brows. He scrutinized the group of milling employees behind Tia. Dismay grew inside him. ''Where *is* Fred?''

Stewy shrugged, repeated the quick scan of the crowd Mac had just done. His own eyes widened. He swore. ''You think he's still in the john?''

Mac released Tia. Stewy and he sprinted for the open bay and scrambled into the building. They arrived in the washroom together. ''Fred!'' Mac shoved inside. Smoke hazed the room, clawed at his eyes. He peered into the single stall. ''He's not here. Try the women's washroom.''

Stewy darted out. Mac met him as he exited the men's.

''He wasn't in there, either.''

''What the hell…?'' Mac's gut boiled with worry. And suspicion. Had Fred set this fire and then disappeared? No. That was ludicrous. He'd have left with Stewy, taken the trucks to the warehouse. Let the whole plant go up in flames. Then where was he?

Tia had followed them. Her eyes were round with anxiety. ''Did you find him?''

''No.'' Mac's nerves ticked. He opened the elevator. It was empty. "We'd better check his desk and Suzanne's office."

The three of them headed back toward the shipping area. As they passed the pile of charred boxes, Mac heard a noise. He froze. Caught Tia by the arm. "What was that?"

Stewy stopped, too. He shook his head. "I didn't hear nothing, dude."

Tia shook her head, too.

Mac gestured them both to silence, then strained to hear another sound. The moan came again. Soft. Almost inaudible. "Over there." He spun toward a mound of blackened, water-damaged cardboard. With the speed of his accelerating pulse, he knocked the top layer aside. On the cold concrete floor lay a hand. Mac grabbed another layer of wet cardboard and heaved it aside. "Get a medic in here."

Tia raced off.

Stewy stood to one side watching Mac in horror. So quick at leaping into action when he'd discovered the fire, he now seemed as incompetent as a statue. "I-is it Fred?"

"Yes."

"Is...is he...alive?"

Mac recalled the low groan, but he didn't like the color of Fred's skin. Before he could answer Stewy, however, Tia and the paramedic, a young woman, arrived. Mac pulled Stewy out of the way. He could feel the young man's shoulders trembling. He knew exactly how Stewy felt. His own insides were mush.

If not for Tia stepping to his side, making him vitally aware of her presence and support, he might drop to the floor and buckle under the heartache ripping at his soul, at his spirit. But she was a constant reminder of what he'd already lost to their nemesis. Giving up was not an option.

The medic was quick and efficient. She checked Fred's airway and breathing, then his vital signs. Her partner arrived with a wheeled stretcher. Together they stabilized Fred. Mac, Tia and Stewy watched like a small audience at a slow-motion movie.

The silence was too much for Mac. "Is he burned?"

The medics lifted Fred onto the stretcher. The woman said, "Doesn't appear to be."

"What happened to him?" Mac felt cold inside and out. "Why is he unconscious?"

She clamped a securing strap across Fred's chest. "Can't say. Could be smoke inhalation. Could be the lump on his head. They'll run tests at the hospital."

Minutes later Fred was in the ambulance. The siren cried through the early afternoon, rushing him to Valley General. Mac's nerves felt raw. His nostrils stung with the stench of smoke. He wanted to hit something again and again and again, until the anger inside him dissipated.

"Should one of us go to the hospital with Fred?" Stewy asked.

"No." Mac couldn't keep the anger from his voice. "We can't do anything for Fred but pray. We have business that needs taking care of right here."

"You want me to shovel these ruined boxes outside?" Stewy rubbed his hands together anxiously. He seemed to need some way to release his pent-up worry. Maybe giving him a few new responsibilities would help.

"No. With Fred down you'll have to take over the shipping department. First thing I need you to do is order more boxes, then get those two trucks and their cargo delivered to the warehouse and unloaded.''

"Done, dude." Stewy's eyes lit up, and for once Mac didn't have to ask him twice. He hurried for the phone.

With Tia at his side Mac strode to the open bay. "Suzanne! Gwen! Will! Nancy!"

The department heads glanced up, caught his gesturing hand and hastened into the loading dock. Suzanne surveyed the smoke damage, wrinkling her tiny nose in disgust. "I overheard one of the firefighters saying if we'd had a sprinkler system in this building, it would have prevented the smoke damage."

Mac swore under his breath. "Yeah, and *that* would have caused unnecessary water damage throughout the rest of the building and shut us down." He bit back his temper, a task that grew more difficult with each passing minute. "Suzanne, your work area will be back up and in operation by clock-in time tomorrow morning. I realize it's only one o'clock, but send your people home for the day. You go, too. See you at the party tonight."

"You're going ahead with the party?" Gwen shook her head, her tawny hair shifting like a pile of silk over her shoulders. "After Fred...?"

Mac turned fierce eyes on Gwen. "Yes, dammit. There's been too much tragedy."

Gwen stiffened as though he'd struck her.

Nancy sniffed. She looked more like a raccoon than ever with her tear-smudged eye makeup. But she seemed calmer. "Grant's right. I, for one, would like to celebrate being alive."

"I second that," Will piped up.

Gwen shot him an annoyed glance.

"Oh, really, Gwennie, you think Fred would be missing this party if he had a choice?" Will's hand rested on his hip.

"No," she conceded. "I suppose not."

"I think the party is just what we all need." Suzanne added her vote. "My staff will appreciate it. And I'm going to tell them now."

As she headed off, Gwen stepped close to "Grant" and flicked his tie intimately. "Save me a dance, tiger."

She gave Tia a look of triumph. "Before I lock up and take off for the day, I'll arrange delivery of new sterile suits."

Gwen sauntered toward the loading dock like a woman expecting to be watched. The tips of Mac's ears warmed. He didn't want to dance with Gwen. Or anyone else. Except, perhaps, Tia. Trouble was, he'd never learned how. Not one step. He supposed his only out was to insist Grant suffered the same social failing. His palms dampened. Would Gwen call him on the lie?

He glanced at Tia. She was staring after Gwen, looking as though she'd like to strangle his vice president. Her emerald eyes burned with something dark. Mac blinked, recognizing the look: jealousy. God, was he nuts? Did he actually have a chance with Tia? Were her recent responses to him as deep as they'd felt? The possibility boosted his spirits, and he determined to find out before the day was done.

"I don't suppose my office will lock itself." Will started for the elevator. "Coming, Nan?"

"Yes." She smiled at Grant and Tia, but the flirting manner she'd exuded the past two days was missing. Mac was grateful.

The sounds of car engines began rending the quiet as the workers left for the day.

Tia moved closer to Mac. "Are you sure it's wise to spend the evening at a party?"

"Yes. Since Buddy and the daytime guard will both be attending, I'd already ordered extra security for tonight."

Tia released a deep breath. "Good."

She gestured at the blackened walls and ceilings, at the conveyor belt heavy with soot and water. "What about this mess?"

His eyes followed hers. And anger pricked his throat. All of his business life, he'd set his mind to something and accomplished it with hard work and imagination. Until now he'd never had to fight for what he wanted. It had come easily. Too easily? No, not everything.

His gut clenched. In many ways he'd let life happen to him. Why? Why had he accepted second to Grant's first? Why had he stood by and watched his brother steal the woman he loved without so much as a single word of protest?

Never again. Life was through rolling over Mac Coy. He caught Tia's arm possessively. "There are companies who specialize in this type of cleanup. Let's go call one."

Chapter Fourteen

It was three o'clock when Mac and Tia arrived at his house. They'd stopped at her apartment long enough for her to gather her clothes for this evening. She'd assured him she would be fine at home alone, that he could pick her up later, but she'd abandoned all protest the moment he'd objected.

That had given him a heady sense of power. Taking charge felt great. Fed his confidence.

She'd been quiet on the drive here, staring at her engagement ring, and he wondered what weighed so heavily on her mind. Was she worried about Fred? The fire? Or was this about losing Grant, first to Gwen, then to a murderer?

He parked near the front of the house. But before he could get out of the car, she touched his arm. "I have to tell you something."

"Sure. Anything." He tried to relax, but every cell in his body seemed taut.

She twisted the ring on her finger, her expression bleak, as though she thought herself despicable. She lifted her head and her gaze met his. "The day Grant died, I was going to break off our engagement."

Mac whistled with surprise. "I'll be damned. Why? Because you suspected he was seeing Gwen?"

"No." She shoved her hair behind her ear. "Well, actually I had felt him withdrawing from me, but that had little to do with my decision. I guess you'll think I'm awful, but Grant swept me off my feet. I was in love with the idea of being in love. It only began dawning on me the past six weeks or so that I wasn't in love with Grant. And a woman should be in love with the man she intends to marry."

Mac gazed deeply into her eyes. There was no mistaking the love in them now. The love and the fear. He didn't know how he knew, but that fear was one of impending rejection. Did she really think he didn't love her in return? Was paradise actually within his grasp? His for the taking?

Hope surged through him. Hope and a tinge of disloyalty. But why should he still feel disloyal to Grant? Grant had obviously, also, been planning to break up with Tia. He'd fallen for Gwen.

Mac stroked a finger down her cheek. Pulled her to him and kissed her delicious mouth. The kiss felt fresh and new, as though barriers were lowering, as though releasing something pure and honest and rare.

A minute later he pulled back, breathless, happy as he'd never been before. "We'll catch cold if we sit out here necking."

"Then let's go inside and neck." She laughed and scrambled out of the car.

A package rested against the door. This one was not a gaily decorated gift from Santa, but rather a large box from the department store where Grant bought most of his clothes. Mac's new suit.

Tia picked up the box. "Let's hope it fits."

"How about a preview?" He unlocked the door. "You show me yours and I'll show you mine."

"Why not?"

Twenty minutes later she watched him descend the stairs from his bedroom. Her heart tripped with love. The realization startled her. No. She mustn't love him. But it was too late. She knew it. Knew it in the way his gaze rolled over her, the way his look, so smoldering and slow, stoked her blood, made her feel as if his fingers were feathering her flesh.

All knowledge of her secret melted like sugar at a simmering heat. She smoothed the new green silk sheath she'd picked up in Taiwan over her hips. Her tongue slipped across her lips.

As he moved closer, she felt herself being drawn to him. He grinned at her. "You approve?"

Oh, yes, her heart answered, dissolving into a puddle of want. *Oh, no,* her head objected, trying to wade through the liquid heat condensing good intentions, solid resolution to a million beads of need. "You look very handsome."

The words came out breathy and warm. He stared at her mouth, and she wanted the kiss he offered. Wanted that, and so much more. He strode toward her. She moved to meet him, unable to resist his lure, knowing she should listen to her reservations, but no longer sure what they were.

Absurdly she noticed his tie was off center. Smiling, she reached for it. Plucked the knot loose. Holding both ends, she tugged him toward her, taking the kiss. He mustn't doubt what she wanted from him. If he pulled back this time, said he couldn't do it…then what?

Would she finally be able to walk away from him,

release this unspoken bond between them? Would she ever?

He dragged her into his arms and pressed his body the length of hers, answering the question of his physical need for her. She moaned against his mouth, and he deepened the kiss with more boldness than he'd ever shown. Heat blew through her, scattering the ashes of her resistance, swirling them into oblivion.

Mac straightened and leaned back. His eyes were dark with ardor, his voice husky, his gaze tender. "I don't just want you, Tia. I love you. I've loved you for a whole year. I should have told you earlier. But I didn't think I had a chance. Especially after Grant came into the picture."

He'd loved her before she met Grant? Tia's heart sang. Just as quickly her throat constricted. Poor Mac. He thought Grant was lucky to have won her. He didn't know fate had stepped in and protected his best interests. If he knew the truth about her, would he feel the same?

She had to know. Now.

"I need you, Tia." He traced her bottom lip with his forefinger. "I need you so."

"Oh, Mac." Her pulse fluttered, her insides quivering with fear. "I need you, too. But I have to tell you something else about me."

He leaned into her. "I don't care what it is."

"But I love you so much I have to tell you—"

"You love me?" He cut her off. The awe in his voice was as thick as rich cream. He let out a joyous yelp, lifted her off her feet and swung her in a small circle.

She tried telling him again, "Mac, I—"

His mouth found hers again and swallowed her

confession, drowning it in her body's lava-hot response to this man, the only man whose kiss could addle her best intentions, her good senses.

Mac swept her up, carried her to his room and lowered her to her feet. He cupped her head gently in both hands as though it were an antique Christmas ornament. Love shone from his turquoise eyes, arrowing straight into that desolate corner of her heart and uncurling the cruel edges, smoothing them into something silken and desired, something she'd craved since childhood.

But the passion she felt for this man had awakened in her woman's body.

She reached for his jacket and skimmed it off his broad shoulders. Next she tossed the tie aside, then began loosening the buttons of his shirt, feeling as though she was loosening the restraints on the love she'd kept pent-up inside, hidden from all, including herself.

She whisked the shirt down his strong arms, the warmth of his skin delicious against her fingertips. Her flesh felt alive, tingling with anticipation. She gazed at his naked chest, mesmerized by its broad expanse, by the dense hair that grew thick between his nipples and trailed down his flat stomach to disappear into his slacks. She couldn't resist touching it, tracing her finger over the hard planes of his belly, until she reached the button that was the last obstacle between her and the treasure of his love.

Mac looked nervous, anxious. He'd made no attempt to undress her. Why? As quickly as she wondered, she recalled his confession: "I...I haven't had...er, any experience with the fair sex." The tenderness she'd felt for him at that admission flooded her anew. She caressed his cheek and gazed at him reassuringly, then took his hand and guided it to the zipper at the back of her sheath.

He swallowed hard, but began tugging the closure open, his hand jittery against every inch of naked flesh he exposed. She brought his hands to her shoulders and together they pushed the fabric aside. She felt the expensive silk pool at her feet. She kicked the dress away.

Mac's gaze began to smolder as he took in her lacy green underwear. She murmured, "The bra unhooks in front."

Mac felt the blood in his groin thumping. The old fear threatened to destroy the moment. He fought to hold off his release. He didn't want to rush. Didn't want to do anything but please this woman who was giving so completely of herself, giving him such pleasure.

But he had no way of knowing whether or not he could return the favor. In truth he didn't even know how. Would she show him—as she was showing him the secret of unfastening her bra? His pulse skidded and leaped. The lacy green fabric parted at his touch and fell away, revealing her ripe, full breasts. His blood sang in his ears and his gaze riveted on the beauty of her. Need throbbed through him.

"It's okay. You can touch me. Taste me."

Mac stiffened, fear keeping his hands curled at his sides.

When he didn't move, she stepped toward him until her hard nipples grazed his chest. He groaned in delicious agony. Her finger slipped inside his slacks. He felt the button give, then the zipper, then she was shoving his slacks and shorts down his legs.

Mac thought he'd explode for sure now. He reached for Tia, kissed her until their tongues danced as one. She pulled back, breathless. As he watched she peeled off her panties, then lay on his bed and beckoned him to join her. "Touch me, Mac. Make me yours in every way."

Oh, yes, that was what he wanted, what he'd dreamed of for a whole year. But as he climbed onto the bed, he felt his control slipping. His need was too powerful. Too long denied. The tips of his ears burned. Led by the passion he could no longer rein in, he moved, instead of beside her, between her legs.

As he plunged into her, he found her moist and taut. The deeper he thrust, the more her body accommodated him, welcomed him, drove him more wild for release. She raised her hips to meet his thrusts. All three of them. Then he climaxed with such speed and force he cried her name aloud.

Mac couldn't look at her. Couldn't bear the disappointment he would see in her beloved eyes. He caught his breath and began easing out of her. His mind scrambled for the proper apology. But he couldn't get the words out of his spasm-choked throat.

He felt Tia's hands on his buttocks. Holding him in place. Effectively stopping his embarrassed retreat. "No," she whispered close to his ear. "Not yet."

He looked at her then. She was smiling, not laughing at him, but beaming like a woman enjoying the moment.

In that instant he felt himself growing hard again. He moaned quietly. He kissed her swollen lips, delved into her sweet mouth. She gave as good as she got, and soon he was thrusting again, slow, deep plunges, she was hot and tight and damp. There was no hurrying. No fear. She shivered beneath him, again and again and again, murmuring his name. Her body contracted around him and deepened his rapture, exciting him higher than he'd thought possible. When the climax came this time, he felt lifted from his old restraints, his old fears, onto a new plane, into a new realm. "Oh, Tia…Tia…Tia!"

He collapsed against her, spent and sated, and grinning like a small child with a new toy. The comparison widened his smile. He stayed joined with her until his breath slowed. Regrettably that came too soon. He rolled off her onto his side, then cradled her in his arms.

When he awoke he found her gazing at him with joy. Her fingers were curled in the hair on his chest. He beamed at her and crooked her hair behind her ear. "How do I love thee…"

His need stirred with life, growing hard against her naked thigh. She sighed and reached for him. Mischief danced in her emerald eyes. "Let me *show* you the ways…"

MAC SEEMED to have gained a new confidence in handling the Porsche. He hummed contentedly as he drove the dark, wet roads toward Maple Valley.

Tia pulled her gaze from his beloved profile. She snuggled into the seat, still feeling as though she was wrapped in his arms, feeling whole for the first time in her life. So this was what it meant to be in love, to be loved. She smiled. The huge hole in her heart had healed bit by bit with every touch of Mac's fingers, with every kiss, with every whispered endearment. She hadn't known making love would be so different from having sex. Hadn't believed her soul and heart could find such fulfillment.

She still reeled with bliss. Mac's innocence and eagerness were heady, made her want him even now. Made her wonder if making love with him every day for the rest of her life would ever be enough.

"It's a little hard to shift gears," Mac said, cutting into her dark musings.

"Oh? I thought you were getting better at it."

"Huh?"

"You're driving is much smoother."

Mac laughed. "I wasn't talking about the car. I meant shifting my mind from us to the subjects of murder and espionage."

"Ah, yes, the party." She sighed. Once again she wished they could ask Grant how to proceed next. What exactly they should look for that would give their nemesis away. "Do you have a plan?"

"I—" His cell phone rang. Mac answered, using Grant's name. He listened, speaking intermittently, the passing streetlights shining on his somber expression. "I see. I see. His heart? How serious? Yes. Well, that's good news, right?"

He told the caller he could be reached at this number if need be and hung up. He smiled at her. "That was the hospital. Fred is regaining consciousness."

"You mentioned his heart—what's going on?"

"Apparently he had a heart attack like Stewy feared. They suspect he hit his head when he collapsed. He has a concussion and his lungs suffered some smoke inhalation. The prognosis is cautious but optimistic." Mac's relief sounded tempered. "The trouble is, boxes don't just start on fire by themselves.

The police will question Fred in the morning. Then they'll come to the plant.''

A SMALL CHEER rang through the banquet room at Wilderness Golf and Country Club when Mac told his employees Fred's condition was improving and the prognosis looked good.

Mac and Tia selected seats at the table with the department heads and their spouses and/or dates. Baby red roses circling chunky white candles served as centerpieces, their delicate hues elegant against the soft white tablecloth.

Tia settled her purse on her chair and glanced around. A trio of musicians, situated near a brick fireplace, played Christmas favorites, a quiet backdrop to the chattering crowd. The room was long and narrow. Someone, likely Bijou, had turned it into a winter wonderland. A pine Christmas tree, twinkling with lights and garlands, stood near the sliding glass door. Its rich aroma mingled with the delicious scents of food wafting from the buffet tables.

Tia hadn't realized she was hungry until this moment. Mac leaned close. "Something to drink?"

"I think we'd better keep our heads." She nodded toward the lineup at the bar. "Even as those around us are losing theirs."

"Good idea. Two club sodas coming up."

"I'm going to cruise by the buffet. I'm ravenous."

He clasped her hand, leaned close again and grinned sexily. "Me, too. But I guess I could use some food first."

A tingle skittered from her head to her toes. She squelched it. Mac might be anticipating a romantic rematch, but she dared not allow it. As it was, she'd be lucky to walk away from him with her sanity intact. It was already too late for her heart.

He squeezed her hand and strolled toward the corner bar.

Tia turned and bumped into Gwen. At first she didn't recognize Grant's girlfriend. Her glasses had been replaced by contacts, her lab clothes by a skimpy red dress that hid neither her deep cleavage nor her shapely thighs. The only thing spoiling the effect she'd apparently meant to create was the angry glare in her intense eyes. "If I can't have him...you'll both be sorry."

She seemed drunk, but Tia wondered if Gwen was a woman scorned or something worse. What exactly was she threatening? "I don't think this is the place—"

"Don't say I didn't warn you." Gwen brushed past Tia and headed straight for the bar and "Grant." Tia's hunger lessened. Playing detective might have stimulated her appetite if the stakes weren't so high. But not knowing their adversary was as effective as a diet pill.

At the buffet Will was filling a plate with roast beef, turkey and ham. He glanced at her, then stepped back and smiled. "Aren't we all aglow tonight? Love in the afternoon? Come on, confirm or deny."

Tia's cheeks heated. If making love with Mac showed on her face to the rest of the room, she could be certain that Gwen would make good on her ominous threat. And if she allowed herself to react to everything that was said to her, instead of making her dialogue with their suspects count for something, she might as well go home right now. The idea was to rattle *them.*

"You're looking pretty dapper yourself." She swept her gaze appraisingly over Will. The ring in his right ear was as golden as his hair, his jacket as dark green as the tree, but she'd never seen anything like his tie. Hand-painted, unless she missed her guess. "Interesting tie."

Will stopped adding cheeses to his plate. His eyes lit up. "Do you really think so?"

"It's incredible. I've never seen one like it."

"Of course not. Which clothiers are offering original Will Holdens?"

"It's your own design?" Tia supposed that shouldn't surprise her. He was, after all, an artist. "Are you selling them?"

"To individuals? Heavens, no."

"To stores?"

"I wish. I can't scrape enough seed money together to get the project off the ground." His mouth twitched slyly. "But that's about to change."

He walked away, leaving Tia staring after him, wondering exactly where Will's money ship was sailing in from. Taiwan or the U.S.? How could she find out without seeming too curious? Without risking her life or Mac's?

Puzzling this, she glanced at the array of foods and once again her hunger called. Deciding to try a bit of everything, she started with the fresh veggies arranged on a silver star-shaped platter. It reminded her of the silver star responsible for the stitches in her forehead. She reached for her bangs to make sure they still covered the bandage.

Suzanne approached with her companion of the evening, a graceful, middle-aged woman. Her mother? Suzanne spoke to the woman in an Asian tongue, the words impossible for Tia to understand, but she didn't need an interpreter to know it had been a warning of some sort. The older woman tensed, lowered her gaze and skirted past Tia as though she reeked of garbage. She headed to the opposite end of the table.

Tia cast a questioning frown at Suzanne. In her shiny black suit, she resembled a miniature panther and was just as skittish. At least around Tia. Was she afraid Tia would see the guilt she couldn't quite hide? Or that she'd ask her again about the factory in Mexico? Suzanne nodded, a curt dip of her sleek head, and followed the other woman to the far end of the table.

Tia went back to filling her plate.

Why had the older woman dashed away from her? Did *she* know something? The thought excited Tia. She stole a surreptitious glance in the direction of the two women. Could she get the older woman alone? And then what? Did the woman even speak English? And if she did, would a mother tell secrets on her daughter?

The sharp tang of cheap perfume—used with an overly generous hand—stole the thought. Bijou, looking like Mrs. Claus in a red velvet outfit with fake white fur trim, bounded up to her.

"How's the food?" Instead of pencils, mistletoe poked from her French roll. Her cheeks were the bright pink of someone who'd had too much to drink.

"I haven't tasted it yet." Tia leaped back to avoid a splash from the glass of red wine Bijou waved at her. "But the spread is one of the nicest I've seen. And it smells delicious. You've done a great job with the party."

"You think?" Bijou didn't look convinced. "Juggling...well, it isn't easy, you know?"

"Juggling?"

"A career, motherhood..."

"Doesn't your husband help?"

Bijou went as pale as the fur trim on her dress. "Do you know my husband?"

Tia retreated a step in surprise and to avoid the wine again. "Why would *I* know him?"

"You fly to Taiwan, someone said. Is that right?"

"Yes, but—"

"Don't mind me." She broke off, a glint of something close to fear in her eyes, and gulped her wine. "I shouldn't drink. Loose lips..."

She swallowed the last of her drink and headed to the bar for another. Tia's stomach clenched. What was Bijou's husband doing in Taiwan? Who was he? How could she find out?

Tia carried her plate back to the table. Frustration settled over her. She had one question after another. But no answers. She was beginning to think this was a waste of time. How could Mac and she unearth a killer at a party? They weren't detectives. They didn't even know what they were looking for.

"Hi, girlfriend."

Tia halted at the sound of the familiar voice. She spun around to greet the first person she was truly glad to see this night. "Ginny, what are you doing here?"

Her best friend beamed at her. "Buddy needed a date and I wasn't doing anything. Besides, I wanted to meet Grant."

For the second time in half an hour, Tia's cheeks burned. She hadn't told Ginny the truth about Grant.

She hated lying to her one true confidante, even a lie of omission. But there was no way she could expose Mac to her best friend when Ginny's brother might be the one who'd tried to destroy him.

She wished it could be otherwise. But until they unmasked Grant's killer or Holly Beary was safely launched, she had to keep the sham alive.

"Yo, dudette, great news about the big guy, huh?" Stewy held a beer bottle by the neck. The only difference between his work duds and his evening clothes was his footwear. He'd traded the logger boots for black Nikes.

Tia introduced Ginny. As Stewy explained to her who the "big guy" was, Tia glanced around the room and found Mac staring at her. Her heart leaped and her throat constricted. He was heading for the table, carrying their drinks. She tightened her grip on her plate and started toward him as though pulled by some force she couldn't see but only feel.

They reached the table at the same time. Mac set the glasses down. Tia slid the plate onto the table and froze. Someone had left Mac a present. Another tiny box. From Santa. For Grant.

Chapter Fifteen

Mac's anger—lulled to sleep in the afternoon of delicious discovery with Tia—awoke like a disturbed dragon. He grabbed the package and ripped the paper off. Several people at the table glanced in his direction. He didn't care. Let them see. Let the one who'd left it reveal himself through his guilt or consternation.

Another Lei Industries box. He tipped the lid off. Inside, resting on a square cotton pad, he found a heart-shaped computer chip. His throat closed. Was this his chip? Or an inferior ripoff?

"Ma—"

He gazed sharply at Tia. She'd almost spoken his name in her distress. Her cheeks reddened as she strove to recover. "Wh-what is it?"

He pushed the box closer for her to see when what he wanted was to storm out, drive straight to the lab and test the chip. But Tia's near giveaway made him think twice. It was one thing to rattle their nemesis, another to invite an attack at the lab. And ducking out of this party early would look suspicious. Would surely draw the wrong person's attention. Better to sneak to the lab after hours tonight.

Tia pushed the box back to him, her face pale as ice. He stared at the chip. What the hell did it mean? Why was someone leaving him these "gifts"? He heard a sharply indrawn breath and glanced up to see Bijou gaping in horror at the Lei Industries box. "What's wrong, Bijou? Did you leave this for me?"

"No." She shook her head, stepping back.

"Did you see who did?"

She pulled her gaze from the box and scanned the party-goers as though expecting some monster to leap out at her. Tears sprang to her eyes and she ran from the room. Mac exchanged a puzzled look with Tia. She touched his wrist. "Let's speak to her."

But when they reached the hallway, they saw her going into the ladies' room. Tia said, "I guess *I'll* speak to her."

Bijou jerked like a startled rabbit when Tia entered and shut the door behind her. She had the shakes. Something was terribly wrong. Tia strode past her and checked the stalls, making sure they were alone.

Then she joined Bijou near the sink. She wet a paper towel and handed it to the distressed woman. "Why don't you get it off your chest?"

Bijou shrugged away from Tia. Her tears abated. "I don't know what you mean."

"Yes, you do. You're obviously frightened of something."

Bijou sniffled and made a face. "Why should I confide in you?"

"Because you look like the secret is killing you."

Bijou laughed without humor. "It's a killer all right."

Tia's nerves jumped. "Does it have anything to do with why you lied on your job application?"

That brought Bijou's chin up and narrowed her eyes. "You know about that?"

Tia nodded.

"Well, you don't know anything." Bijou glanced in the mirror, wiped beneath her eyes with the wet paper towel, then straightened a sprig of mistletoe. Her expression collapsed. "My whole life is a lie."

Suddenly Tia wasn't so sure she liked being alone with this woman. She edged toward the door. "A...a lie?"

Bijou gnawed at her thumbnail. "Martin Lei—fifth son of Hai Lei, CEO of Lei Industries—is my husband."

Whatever Tia had expected her to say, it wasn't this. Her mouth dropped open.

"That's right." Bijou nodded.

"Does, er, did Mac know?"

"Oh, God, no." Bijou turned toward her now, a crazed gleam in her aqua eyes. "No one knows."

Tia bumped into the door. With her hands behind her she grappled for the knob.

Bijou dug into her purse and withdrew a long metal nail file. She shook the sharp pointed end at Tia. Tia's pulse skipped. But the other woman made no move toward her. Instead, she grew very still. "I have no doubt Martin would kill me if he could find me."

Tia's mouth was as dry as angel hair. "He abused you?"

"Oh, yes. But as far as he's concerned, I committed the worse crime—I took our son and fled to the States. He's been looking for me ever since."

For a half second Tia wondered what it would feel like to have both her parents love her so much they would fight over her. Look to the ends of the earth for her. She couldn't even imagine such a thing. But her heart squeezed for Bijou's son. No matter that she was trying to protect him from an abusive father, the boy would not escape without emotional scars. "It's fairly easy to find people these days. How have you managed to elude him for four years?"

"I changed my name, the color of my hair and the color of my eyes with contacts. I gained thirty pounds on purpose and started dressing like a woman with no sense of style or taste." Bijou sniffled again and blew her nose hard into the paper towel. "It's an effective disguise, don't you agree?"

"Yes." Tia released the doorknob and studied Bijou as though seeing her for the first time. Was she lying? If not, Tia supposed becoming a dumpy eccentric with a weird name was a good way to hide in plain sight. But there was one thing she didn't understand. "Why are you working for a competitive toy company?"

"In order to keep tabs on Martin. I know what he's up to, where he goes, who he sees." She scraped the file over her thumbnail. "It's the only way I'll know ahead of time if my cover is blown."

Tia didn't know whether or not to believe this tale. Whether or not she was staring at the fox in the henhouse. She was only certain that Mac was not going to be happy to discover he might have one of Hai Lei's daughter-in-laws on his payroll. "Did you leave that gift for Grant?"

"No. And I don't know who did. But it scared the hell out of me, I can tell you that. What's going on?"

Tia shook her head and shrugged. *That* was what she and Mac wanted to know.

Two giggling women barged through the door, then stopped as they saw Tia and Bijou. "Oh, is there a lineup?"

"No," Tia assured them. She turned to leave.

Bijou grabbed her by the arm.

Tia flinched.

Bijou said, "What I told you—our secret, okay?"

"Of course." But Tia had no intention of keeping this from Mac. She needed to talk to him now. As she hurried into the hallway, she collided with Nancy Rice. Nancy apologized, but seemed so flustered Tia wondered if she'd been eavesdropping.

"NICE PARTY, Mr. Coy." Buddy Gibson eyed the box and wrapping paper. It seemed to make him nervous. He was the seventh of their suspects made uncomfortable by the sight of this present.

"Do you know who left this for me, Bud?" Mac asked.

"No, not me." He lifted his hands in innocence, but his denial came too quickly. He knew something, but what? Bud turned toward the woman standing beside him. "This is my sister, Ginny."

Tia's best friend. Mac switched his attention to the pert redhead. Dressed all in silver, her fiery hair in short spikes atop her head, she resembled a glittery seasonal candle. She was giving him a head-to-toe inspection. He could swear she didn't quite approve of him. He bit back a smile. As far as he knew, she thought he was Grant and she probably knew Tia was ready to break up with his twin.

What would she think when she learned the truth, learned Tia would be marrying him, instead of Grant?

The thought gave him the first sense of comfort he'd felt since their afternoon of lovemaking.

In the background the trio played "Jingle Bell Rock." His gaze fell to the chip. He dropped the lid back on the box. His mood soured. Despite his tender memories of the day and his anticipation of a future with Tia, he couldn't get caught up in the gay music or laughter or chatter all around him. His love for this season diminished with every hour his brother's killer walked free to wreak more havoc.

"Where's Tia?" Ginny asked.

"Ladies' room." He glanced toward the hallway, wondering what was taking her so long. Had he left her to face the devil alone? Acid burned his stomach.

"Then I'll get a cocktail while I'm waiting," she said. "Buddy, you want another beer?"

"Yeah, sure. Thanks, sis." Bud glanced at Mac. "T and Ginny've been friends since they were kids."

"She told me." Mac absently tapped the Lei Industries box.

"I'll bet." Bud stared at Mac's bouncing finger. "She tell you anything about me?"

"A little." Mac gave him an ominous scowl. Maybe he should go find out if she was okay.

"Yeah, I'll bet." Bud looked as though his tie was choking him. "But she probably didn't rat on herself, did she?"

"What?" Mac gathered the box and dropped it into his coat pocket. It settled there like a stone.

Bud was scowling. "I'll bet she didn't tell you she was arrested for selling company secrets when she worked for Crimble Industries, did she?"

"What?" Mac gaped at Bud. Was this the secret

Tia hadn't been able to tell Grant but had wanted to tell him? His throat dried. "She went to jail?"

"Nooo. No, jail for *her,*" he said bitterly. "The charges were dropped. But that don't give her the right to shoot off her mouth about me."

"Tia didn't say anything negative about you, Bud. Just mentioned you were the kid brother of her best friend."

"Oh, jeez." Bud stumbled up from the table. Sweat popped out on his face. "I gotta tell you something—"

"Grant, I think this is our dance," Gwen interrupted, and Bud clamped his mouth shut as though his life depended on it. Gwen gave him a dirty look that sent him fleeing after his sister. She plunked her full wineglass on the table next to the torn wrapping paper, then leaned over Mac. "Come on, sugar, let's show the folks how it's done."

"Gwen, you've had too much to drink. And I'm not in a dancing mood."

"It's her, isn't it?" Gwen swayed on her feet.

Mac cringed at the scene she was making, but he felt sorry for his old friend. Apparently she'd loved Grant. This ruse he and Tia were perpetrating was hardest on her, and if she was another innocent victim in this mess, she'd suffer a worse heartache when she learned the truth. "Please, just sit down."

"It *is* her, isn't it?" She raised her voice. "You really love her?"

He murmured, "Yes."

"Beep. Wrong answer." A spaghetti strap had slipped off one of Gwen's shoulders, revealing more than he cared to see of her. He reached for the strap.

She slapped his hand away. "You'll rue the day you messed with me, Grant Coy."

She tossed her drink in his face. Mac jerked back. Will let out a gasp, then rushed to his aid with a napkin. Suzanne went to Gwen's aid and got the same brushoff as Mac. Gwen stormed away. Suzanne turned to Mac and tugged him out of his soiled jacket, dabbing it dry with a second napkin. Red wine dripped from his chin down the front of his shirt. Felt sticky. He hurried to the men's room to wash it off.

Nancy stood near the ladies'. She straightened, looking as guilty as if Mac had caught her defiling a nativity scene. What was she up to?

TIA AND GINNY were standing beside the table chatting when Mac returned. Tia gazed at his shirt in horror. "What happened?"

"Gwen."

"Oh."

"Oh?" Ginny inquired.

"Long story," Tia told her. "Later, okay?"

"Sure."

Mac stepped closer to Tia. "I've had about all the gaiety I can stand for one night. How about you? Want to leave?"

"It looks like things are breaking up, anyway. And we do need to compare notes."

Again Ginny raised an eyebrow. "What are you two up to?"

"Ginny, I'll tell all, soon. I promise."

"Okay. I have something I should have told you sooner, too." That worried expression was back in her eyes. She bade them good-night and went in search of her brother.

"After we talk I want to go to the lab and test this chip," Mac said. This time he would give her the chance to tell him about her past. This time he would listen and assure her it meant nothing to him, *show her* exactly how little it mattered. Desire teased his groin.

Mac gathered his jacket and slipped it on. He reached into the pocket for the car keys. A chill tripped along his spine. He whispered to Tia, "It's gone. The box containing the chip. Someone stole it."

He scanned the room, seeking any of their suspects making a stealthy departure. But party-goers seemed to be leaving in droves—as though everyone was guilty. He considered calling them all back, demanding to know which of them had taken it. He grimaced. Just as he'd demanded to know which of them had left it? Fat lot of good that had done.

He found the hostess and settled the bill, then guided Tia out to the car.

By the time he started his car, the parking lot had emptied. The temperature had dipped below freezing and the roads were slick. Keeping an eye out for black ice, Mac listened as Tia related her conversation with Bijou.

His frustration and anger twisted like ribbons in the wind. He cursed his trusting nature. First thing tomorrow he and his head of sales would be having a long conversation. But for now he felt more disheartened than ever. "The party was a joke. Nothing we learned tonight has put us one step closer to finding Grant's killer."

His cell phone rang. He answered, "Grant Coy."

"Mr. Coy, it's Bud Gibson. I'm at the plant, sir. I think you should come down here right away."

"What?"

"The security team you hired have taken off. I found the place wide open."

Chapter Sixteen

"What!" Mac's blood ran cold. He swore.

"What's wrong?" Tia asked, the anxiety in her voice matching the tension gripping him.

Mac couldn't answer her yet. "Bud, what are you doing there?"

"I guess I should have told you right out, instead of taking the coward's way," Bud said. "But after Mac died, I didn't know who my friends were."

"I don't know what you're taking about."

"I came back to the plant tonight to return the chip. I'm the one who's been leaving you those gifts from Santa."

"You? Why?"

"Because Mac Coy was good to me. He gave me a chance to turn over a new leaf and I owed him. A couple weeks ago I had my sister bring me back one of those Lei Industries bears and several little boxes. She flies to Taiwan with T, you know?"

"What were you trying to do with them?"

"I was trying to make you realize someone in this place is crooked. Trouble is, I don't know who. But Mac told me you were a clever detective. So I figured with some prompting you'd try and figure it out."

"Where did you get the chip?"

"From the bear in your office. I came here tonight to put it back. That's when I found the security guards gone. The plant unlocked. I'm going to check out the place now. I'll call you back soon."

He hung up.

"Something's going on at the plant." Mac stomped harder on the gas. The Porsche lurched ahead like a trusty steed carrying the good guys to the rescue. But would they be too late? His heart thundered in his chest. He related Buddy's conversation to Tia.

She blew out a taut breath. "So that's what Ginny's been too nervous to tell me. She probably thought he had her smuggling drugs into the country."

"Somebody sent the security team away."

Tia gasped. "Who could do that?"

"Gwen is the only one besides me who has the authority."

"Do you think she's the killer?"

"I hope not. Bud's in there without a weapon."

"Should we call the police?"

"Not yet." He didn't want the police interfering if it wasn't necessary. "Let's see what's going on first."

Tia exhaled. "Bud swore to me he was trying to turn himself around. You've been a good influence on him, Mac. Made him feel like he could overcome his background."

Mac smiled at the compliment, but decided this might not be the best moment to mention what Bud had told him about *her* background.

The driving was tense, through busy roadways, over slick pavement. His nerves were raw by the time he pulled into the parking lot near the shipping bay. He braked, cut the engine and placed his hand over

Tia's. "Stay here. Please. If I'm not back in ten minutes, call 911."

Tia waited exactly three minutes. Each second felt like an eternity. She got out of the car and slipped into the building, the same way she'd seen Mac enter. The only light on the first floor issued in a dim glow from the product room. Suzanne Chang's area. The bite of disinfectant filled the air. Only a tinge of smokiness remained.

Her nerves jumping, Tia crossed the concrete floor. Her steps echoed in her ears. Where was Mac? She dared not call his name. No telling who might overhear. She called softly, "Grant?"

The sudden hum of machinery riveted her. She jolted and spun toward the noise. The conveyor belt. Why would it be running? Fear licked through her. She pivoted. Her gaze winged into every shadowed corner. "Grant?"

Still no answer. Her gaze moved unwittingly back to the conveyor belt. Through the flapped opening something began to appear. Something large. She stepped closer. A body. Tia froze. Horror chilled her blood. Gwen. A dark patch stained the vivid red dress. Gwen's bright eyes stared at the ceiling. Seeing nothing. Dull now. Dead.

A scream ripped from Tia. She wanted to run. Her legs were leaden. She stumbled back and bumped into something solid. A man. Her heart stopped. "G-Grant?"

"Why don't we join the guys upstairs." Strong fingers dug into her arm and a gun was rammed against her temple.

"Fred?" Shock waves rolled through her. "But… you're in the hospital."

He laughed, a mean-spirited chortle. "That was my little joke on your stupid fiancé. I'm the one who called him earlier tonight to give him an update on my 'condition.'" He laughed again.

The vision of Fred being worked on by the paramedics filled her head. "But you were unconscious."

"Faked it."

She was incredulous. The paramedics would have known. She dredged up the memory and recalled the female medic saying she didn't know why Fred was unconscious. Had she suspected he wasn't? "But the bump on your head? You couldn't have faked that."

"A stroke of luck I used to my advantage. I banged my head earlier loading those damned bears into the truck. I set fire to the boxes and then I just hid out in the john until the flames were extinguished, blackened my face a little and climbed under some charred cardboard."

"But…why? Why did you kill these people?"

He tightened his grip on her arm.

Tia winced in pain.

He snarled, "You don't know what it's like, struggling through life in a dead-end job you hate, never having what you want, always settling."

"You're wrong. I know exactly what that's like. But I wouldn't kill anyone."

He jammed the gun harder against her temple. Tia's throat tightened. He growled into her ear, "You haven't had your dream snatched from you time and time again. You're too young to know the feeling that your life is slipping away. My time is now. Or never. Nobody is taking this cartoon from me. It's my last shot at making it big."

"I'm sure Mac would have given you the rights to

the cartoon.'' Her voice came out in a squeak. ''If you'd asked.''

He laughed again. ''You don't understand how much money is involved. He'd have squandered the profits on little kids—same as he had since I'd known him. He couldn't even get this company into the black. Money wasn't important to him like it is to me. He'd always had it. He never knew the hell of being poor.''

''So you killed him?''

''Ah, well, I hadn't planned on that, hadn't planned on anyone dying, but he caught me in Bijou's office talking to my connection at Lei Industries. He was going to turn me over to the police.''

Tia couldn't speak from fear. He shoved her into the elevator and pushed the button for the third floor. ''Lei is giving me full rights to the cartoons for *their* bear. And I've got an agent in New York shopping my proposals.'' He grinned at her as though undressing her. A wooden matchstick poked between his fleshy lips. ''Too bad I don't have time to sample your wares, but I've got a plane to catch. While you and your fiancé are walking through the Pearly Gates, I'll be winging my way to Taiwan to seal the deal.''

The elevator glided past the second floor.

Pearly Gates? Had he already killed Mac, too? Her heart hurt so much at the thought she couldn't breathe. Couldn't bring herself to ask. ''You broke into Grant's offices, didn't you? Why?''

''Because I found the strangest thing in Mac's pocket—keys to Quell Inc. and one of those credit-card things that bypasses a security system. Made me wonder if he'd secretly gotten wind of the Lei deal and involved his brother the snoop.''

Her heart hitched. Then he really hadn't known it was Grant he killed. She glared at him. "You hit me on the head."

He gnawed the wooden matchstick. "You got in my way."

Her bluster withered. She shivered. "Is that what Gwen did?"

"She showed up when I was trying to figure out how to get past the security team." He shifted the matchstick to the other side of his mouth and grinned slyly. "She sent them home. I waited until they split, then found her in the lab. She wasn't about to let me take that precious chip of hers, but I need those chips to cinch the deal with Lei. Without Mac's brainbaby, their bear is a no go."

The elevator doors swung open. A light shone in Mac's office. As they approached, she saw him. Her lungs filled and her pulse leaped with hope. Then she realized he was kneeling beside a man sprawled on the floor. Buddy. Blood oozed from his forehead and his face was the color of cream cheese. Her heart dropped to her toes. Poor Buddy. He had tried reforming and been killed for his effort. *Oh, Ginny.*

Fred steered her into the office. Mac's head jerked up. Shock washed his expression. And fear. His gaze locked on the gun trained on Tia. The tips of his ears reddened, and she knew it was from anger. He started to stand, his fists curling at his sides. "Fred? You? You killed my brother?"

"Oh, Mac, don't be mad." The tinny voice of Holly Beary issued from the shelf behind Fred.

Fred jerked as though he'd been hit. He released his hold on Tia and spun around, looking confused. "Mac?"

Tia knew this was their only chance. She smashed her fist on the hand holding the gun. It fired, but flew from his grip.

Mac dove past her, tackling Fred. Tia scrambled for the gun. In trembling hands she aimed it at the struggling men. "Stop fighting or I'll shoot."

But Mac was too angry to listen. He rammed his fist into Fred's fleshy belly, then once more into his jaw. Fred groaned and collapsed to the floor. Out cold.

Sirens sounded outside. In minutes the factory would be overrun with police.

Tia laid the gun on the worktable and ran to Mac. He threw his arms around her. Breathless, he said, "It's over, love."

Tia blanched. It was more over than he knew.

DAWN POKED GRAY through the blinds in Mac's office, the perfect backdrop for Tia's mood. She and Mac had spent the whole night at police headquarters. Her body ached. Her mind felt fuzzy. But the red tape and paperwork created because of Mac's lie about Grant's death were being handled. Expedited.

The district attorney had assured them the only painting Fred Vogler would be doing for the rest of his life would be behind bars.

Buddy Gibson would have his chance at a new, honest future. He'd been lucky. The bullet had cut a swath across the top of his skull, but hadn't entered his brain. He'd have a permanent reminder, an ugly scar, but he would mend quickly.

She wished her own wound were as easily healed. But as the night wore on, as each detail was resolved or started toward resolution, the time drew closer for her talk with Mac. Their final talk. Her heart felt as though it were shredded.

She wanted to disappear, but she wouldn't. She wouldn't let Mac think she'd left because she didn't love him. He wouldn't suffer the doubts she'd lived with all her life. And she loved him so much she had to tell him the truth.

It was a morning of truths. Suzanne Chang had admitted there was no factory in Mexico. The bears were being made in Seattle. In the Asian district. But not in the sweatshop Tia had feared.

Through her mother, Suzanne found a group of women needing to work from home. They were fast and efficient. They produced a great product, under the allowed budget, yet all were well compensated and could work their own hours and in comfortable circumstances. Plus, shipping costs for transporting the bears to the plant were kept low.

She hadn't told Mac because most of the seam-stresses were her relatives. She feared he'd disap-prove.

Mac not only approved, he was relieved.

He closed the door behind Suzanne, and for the first time in eight hours, Tia and Mac were alone.

He looked weary. Dark circles underscored his eyes, and there was a tightness to his mouth. Besides Grant, he'd lost Gwen, his vice president, head of electronics and longtime friend. He'd lost Fred, who'd run the shipping department. And he'd lost a lot of illusions about all the people who worked for him. He'd had a hell of a week. She was about to make it worse. The pain in her chest doubled. Hurting him was the last thing she wanted and the only thing she could do.

Mac ran his hand over his head. He needed a shave. Somehow it made him more vulnerable. "Enough of the bears are in the warehouse to get the shipment under way. The launch won't be as grand as planned, but Lei Industries is no longer a player. Their bear is history."

Tia smiled. Under normal circumstances she'd have cheered loud and long. It was a huge success for the children of the world.

And Holly Beary would be a success for Mac.

She crossed the room to him and reached for his hand. His wonderful hand. She stifled the image of that hand on her, the ache for that hand on her. She placed her engagement ring into his palm. "This belongs to Gwen. I'm only sorry I couldn't give it to her when she was alive. More sorry that we couldn't ease her mind about Grant's love."

He nodded. "She's with Grant now. It's not the way it should have been, but at least he's not alone."

Tears filled her eyes and she saw that his, also, glistened with grief. Pure, guilt-free grief for Grant. He reached tender fingers to wipe the dampness from her cheek. "At least *I'm* not alone."

His words scared her. Tia pulled back. Her heart breaking for him. For them both. "Mac, I have to tell you…"

He caressed her jaw. "I already know about Crimble Industries."

Tia tensed. "What?"

"Bud told me at the party last night."

"That rat." She grimaced, her childhood animosity roused. "To think I felt sorry for him."

"He said the charges were dropped."

"The charges were trumped-up. My boss was the

one selling company secrets. I was young and naive, and when I stumbled onto what he was doing, I was easily framed.''

"Bud said you didn't go to jail.''

She made a face. "Not because the police didn't try to put me there. They invaded my home like thieves, robbing me forever of my sense of security.'' She hugged herself. "It was an ugly experience.''

"Is that why your apartment resembles a motel room?''

"Yes. If anyone ever paws through my possessions again, there's nothing to touch that I care about.''

Mac looked as though he wanted to touch her so she would never question how much he cared...about her. Her pulse wobbled. He frowned and took a step toward her. "I don't understand why you didn't feel you could tell Grant this.''

"I did tell him.'' She moved a step backward, her mouth drying.

He looked completely confused. He stepped toward her again. "But I thought—''

She retreated again. "Please, let me finish.''

"Let me hold you.'' He came closer.

"No.'' She held her hands up to stop him. "I don't think I could get through this if you did.''

"Tia, nothing could be so bad.''

"This is.''

"I don't care what you've done.''

"Oh, it's nothing I've done.'' With a trembling hand she gestured toward the worktable. "Please, Mac, sit down.''

They took chairs across from one another. Tia clasped her hands in front of her to stop the quaking. "Being given up at birth, I've spent my whole life feeling unwanted. Unworthy. The near miss with the couple when I was eight reinforced my sense that something was terribly wrong with me. If my own mother and father didn't want me, how could anyone else?''

She drew a steadying breath and crooked her hair behind her ear. But her hand continued to shake and she folded it back with the other. ''Then Grant came into my life and I thought I'd found love at long last. When we got engaged I started wondering if I was wrong about why my parents had given me up for adoption. Maybe they were looking for me, too. Maybe they'd want to come to my wedding.''

She nearly choked on the thought of how naive she'd been. She forced herself to go on. ''My foster mother, Molly Bowen, helped me track down my birth mother. I found her a month ago. She lives, ironically enough, in North Seattle—a twenty-minute drive from where I grew up.''

Mac leaned toward her, his hands covering hers. ''And was she glad to see you?''

''No.'' The word choked from Tia. She could still see the hatred in her mother's eyes. The revulsion. Bile climbed her throat. ''She never wanted to see me. She said I was the Devil's seed. A child conceived in rape.''

Mac scowled and swore. He gripped her hands more tightly, ignoring her attempts to pull back. ''How could she blame you for that?''

Tia lifted her eyes to his and shook her head, fighting the self-pity aroused by her bitter memories. She'd felt miserably ashamed these past four weeks since learning the truth, as though she'd brought the violence on her mother. Through Mac's love, she now understood that the rape wasn't her guilt to carry. She was as much a victim as her mother. More, even. "I've never told anyone, Mac. Not Molly, or Ginny, or Grant. But I had to tell you."

"It doesn't matter to me. I don't care where you came from. I just thank God you came to me."

And she thanked God for sending her Mac. For letting her experience true love—even for this short time. "I'm not here for you, Mac. Don't count on me or build a world around me. I can't be your future or your wife or anything."

"You don't mean that." His expression blackened. "You can't give up on us because your mother didn't want you."

"No." At least now she knew the wholeness of feeling wanted and needed and loved. The old wound in her heart had healed, but a new one was opening. "You love children, Mac. You'll want kids of your own."

"Yes." He swallowed hard. "With you."

"Not with me, Mac." Tears clogged her throat. "My father is a rapist. In itself that's bad enough, but what if he's a serial rapist? A murderer? What if he's crazy? His blood runs in my veins. I can't pass that on to children. I won't."

He looked as though she'd driven a stake through his heart. "Then we'll adopt."

Her heart swelled with love for this man. If only she could believe it would be enough for him. But she couldn't risk his one day changing his mind. She reached out and touched his cheek. "You deserve a whole woman. Someone who's sure of herself, someone who can give you joy and love. I'm not that woman. I never was and I never will be.''

He lurched to his feet and smacked the table. "You're wrong! I'll make you see."

"Oh, Mac, you almost did...and for that I will be forever grateful." Her gaze traced his face with all the tenderness she felt for him.

She would always remember the look in his eyes now, would always remember the touch of his hands, as if she was something or someone precious, treasured.

But she had to let him go.

As her consolation, she knew Mac would go on to find love with someone else, and he would do it with confidence because she'd helped him see he could. Of course he would lose that innocence she adored, spend that joy of discovery she treasured with another.

But he would eventually find happiness, and that was what mattered. As she stood, a tear rolled from her eyes. Why was she weeping? She'd always known she'd leave his life the moment Holly Beary was safely on its way to stores across the country.

He stepped to her, caught her hands again. "I'm not letting you walk out of my life."

"Don't try to stop me, Mac." She tugged her hands free. "You can't change my history. Launch your toy. Bury your brother. Grieve for him and Gwen. When the pain in your heart begins to lessen, you'll see this is for the best."

He grabbed her. Hugged her to him. She clung to him, cried with him, then pushed from his arms and left.

Chapter Seventeen

The next two weeks passed in a blur of grief, heartache and activity for Tia. The holiday season provided her with extra work, extra flights to keep her out of Seattle, extra stressed-out passengers to keep her mind off her own problems. She was too weary each night to do more than drop into dreamless sleep.

Every morning she'd awaken hoping this would be the day she'd stop loving Mac. But every morning she'd awaken missing him more, loving him more.

She'd seen him three times since the day she'd walked out of his office. Once at Grant's funeral and twice on TV in interviews celebrating the huge success of Holly Beary. Each time Nancy Rice was glued to his side. Tia had expected Nancy and Mac might eventually end up together, but seeing it happen hurt as nothing ever had.

And now it was Christmas Eve. She and Ginny trudged through the packed concourse toward the airport exit. The flight back from Taiwan had been routine. But Tia could barely drag her wheeled flight bag. She felt like sleeping for a week.

Only one good thing had come from the mess with Holly Beary. Tia had finally told Ginny the truth about her parentage. She didn't know why she'd kept it from her for so long. Maybe if she'd told her sooner, she'd have discovered sooner that the tragedy suffered by her birth mother wasn't her fault. She'd have found out Ginny wouldn't shun her. She should have known that, should have trusted her best friend. But terror of another rejection had kept her silent.

Tia stuffed her bag into the taxi and hugged her friend. "I'll be fine, Ginny. Christmas has never been my holiday. You know?"

"Yeah. I know." Ginny stepped back. "Call me tomorrow."

Tomorrow, Tia thought as she approached her apartment door, was just another day in the life of Tia Larken. At least, inside this door, she could shut out the rest of the world and its holiday revelers, its celebrations, its decorations. All the reminders of how lonely and miserable this season made her feel. Tonight her barren apartment would suit her mood to a T. She unlocked the door. Anxious to get inside.

The interior was swathed in darkness, but it wasn't as cold as it ought to be. Had she left the heat on when she'd taken off on the last flight? God help her, her electric bill would be enormous. She hit the light switch and froze.

The apartment looked like a store specializing in Christmas merchandise. Every corner held something festive: scented candles, wreaths of greenery and holly, twinkling lights, foil snowflakes over her kitchen table. Her gaze fixed on the bushy Douglas fir against the window, hung with what appeared to be miniature toys. There were even presents under the tree.

Who had done this? Ginny? She glanced at the coffee table. Two champagne flutes rested next to her silver ice bucket and an unopened bottle of Dom Perignon. A single present the size of a sheet of paper sat beside them.

She hadn't closed the door and knew she could reach it before anyone could catch her. "Who's here?"

"Hi, Tia. Let's play." The voice came from the kitchen. She glanced up and saw Holly Beary propped on the counter.

She took a step toward it. Fascinated. "Did you say something to me?"

The teddy bear answered, "I love you, Tia."

"And so do I." Mac slowly rose from behind the counter.

Her knees wobbled with relief and something she couldn't acknowledge. She pointed at the toy. "How did you...?"

Mac grinned, reaching into the heart of the bear and extracting the red computer chip. "How did I get this to react to your voice?"

She nodded.

"Oh, no." He shook his head. "That's *my* secret."

Mac left the teddy bear on the counter and came out of her kitchen. Her pulse quickened. He wore blue jeans and a white dress shirt with the sleeves rolled to the middle of his strong forearms. He looked even handsomer than he had two weeks ago. His hair was slightly longer and he'd replaced the contacts with a thin-rimmed, attractive pair of glasses, yet he remained clean shaven.

Gone was the "Grant" visage, but he no longer slouched. He walked with a new air of confidence, apparently comfortable at last in the skin of Mac Coy.

Her heart beat so hard she could hear it. She forced a smile, gesturing toward the room. "You did all this?"

"I think you need to learn to appreciate Christmas."

God, this man was so sweet she wanted to cry. "Mac, please, this is really nice, but it's not going to change my mind about us."

"Perhaps not. But I got you a Christmas present and then I saw you had no tree to put it under. And this is such a great present, it just cried out for a tree."

He moved closer and she wanted to run into his arms. It took every ounce of willpower she had to resist.

"Mac, I didn't get you anything."

"Well, you didn't know you'd be seeing me."

"No, and I don't want you to give me a present."

"Why don't you look at it first?" He sat on her sofa and patted the cushion beside him. "Then if you don't want it…I won't ask you to keep it."

She didn't want to sit next to him. Didn't want to play out their breakup scene again. She'd been reliving that every day since it had happened. But she could see he wouldn't leave unless she humored him. She sank onto the sofa. "Oh, all right. What is it?"

"Open it and see." He placed the gaily wrapped box on her lap. Then he lifted the champagne bottle from the ice bucket and popped the cork.

The sound jarred her frayed nerves. "Mac, I don't think you should have opened that. We won't be celebrating—"

"Well, I'm thirsty and champagne is as good as anything for a dry throat." He filled both glasses, then settled back onto the sofa beside her.

The room smelled of the cinnamon candles scattered on every table. And of pine from the tree. And of Mac's aftershave. Her blood hummed. She lifted the gift-box lid with a jittery hand. Reposing on a sheet of Santa-covered tissue paper was the photo of an older man, a black-and-white print of someone she didn't know or recognize. She raised her gaze to Mac. He was grinning at her. Anxious. "Who is this?"

"That is a fellow by the name of John Thomas Merrick. His friends call him J.T."

She shook her head at Mac. "I don't get it. How is this a present for me?"

"J.T. is your father."

Her throat closed. "What?"

"While you've been flying all over Asia, I've been busy, too." He was still grinning.

"Yes, launching the teddy bear." Romancing Nancy. Decorating this apartment. Finding her father? She shook the photograph at him. "How?"

"I went first to your foster mother. She told me the name of your birth mother. I went to see her and we had a long talk."

"I'll bet that was pleasant," she said sarcastically.

"Not particularly. But I made her realize I wouldn't leave without the name of your father." His ears reddened. "I can be persistent."

Despite the knot in her stomach, she smiled. But her nerves stole the warmth as quickly as it came. "Where did you find him?"

"In Kent."

"So close," she whispered.

"Yes. He's been there since he got out of jail."

"He went to jail for rape." A sob caught in her

throat. She braced herself for the worst. "Just tell me, Mac."

"Your mother's family had him arrested for statutory rape. He was twenty at the time. Your mother told him she was eighteen. She was sixteen. He thought they were consenting adults. He thought they would marry. When she found out she was pregnant, she knew her strict Baptist parents would disown her. Or worse. So she cried rape. J.T. went to jail. And you were given up for adoption."

Teenage love gone terribly wrong? God, how she'd like to believe that, but what man accused of rape wouldn't try excusing himself the same way? "Did *he* tell you that?"

"Yes." Mac nodded. "So I visited your mother a second time. Eventually she confirmed the story."

Tia could barely take in what he was telling her. "My father is not a serial rapist," she said, having to hear the words, the acquittal of all charges, out loud.

"No."

"He's not a murderer." She accepted the glass of champagne from Mac. Her mouth was so dry she could barely swallow.

"He's not crazy."

"No, nor did he rape your mother."

"But he went to jail."

"And he's been looking for you ever since he got out."

Tia began to shake. "Looking for me?"

"Your mother wouldn't tell him anything about you. Least of all how to find you." Mac touched her hair as though he'd been longing to for years. "It's impossible to find someone without anything to go on."

Tia swallowed more champagne. The bubbles seemed to be filling the hole in her heart. She wasn't the child of the Devil. She was wanted by one of her parents. Had always been wanted. Tears of joy welled in her eyes, ran hot down her cheeks. She touched Mac's hand. "You've given me my father, Mac…"

The enormity of it stole her voice.

"Oh, J.T. isn't all your family," Mac said. "You've got a stepmom, two half brothers and a half sister. If you want them."

"If I want…" she choked out. Her heart felt as though it were swelling from a tiny seed to a flowering rose. "I want."

"I thought you might." His voice was husky as he caressed her damp cheek. "They're expecting us tomorrow. For Christmas dinner."

"Us?" Her dry throat required another swallow of champagne. "Aren't you spending the day with Nancy?"

"Nancy? Nope. I think she's doing something with Will. She's grown very fond of him since he saved her from the fire."

"Will? I would never have taken him for a *ladies'* man."

"Me, neither, but we were both wrong. You should see the two of them together. And believe it or not, since I gave him his bonus, he's stopped whining about money. He even gave me a great tie for Christmas."

Tia burst out laughing. Mac took her glass, set it on the table beside his own and opened his arms. There was no more resistance in Tia. She dove at him. Laughing, Mac wrapped his arms around her. "God, but I've missed you, woman."

"I've missed you, too."

He leaned back and gazed at her. "Really?"

"Really." She stared at his mouth. That wonderful mouth. "Maybe you should show me how much you've missed me."

He grinned wryly. "Only if you promise you're not *toying* with my affection."

Tia lifted her lips toward his. "Mac, my love for you is the real McCoy."

Take 2 bestselling love stories FREE

Plus get a FREE surprise gift!

Special Limited-Time Offer

Mail to Harlequin Reader Service®

3010 Walden Avenue
P.O. Box 1867
Buffalo, N.Y. 14240-1867

YES! Please send me 2 free Harlequin Intrigue® novels and my free surprise gift. Then send me 4 brand-new novels every month. Bill me at the low price of $3.34 each plus 25¢ delivery and applicable sales tax, if any.* That's the complete price, and a saving of over 10% off the cover prices—quite a bargain! I understand that accepting the books and gift places me under no obligation ever to buy any books. I can always return a shipment and cancel at any time. Even if I never buy another book from Harlequin, the 2 free books and the surprise gift are mine to keep forever.

181 HEN CH7J

Name _____ (PLEASE PRINT)

Address _____ Apt. No. _____

City _____ State _____ Zip _____

This offer is limited to one order per household and not valid to present Harlequin Intrigue® subscribers. *Terms and prices are subject to change without notice. Sales tax applicable in N.Y.

UINT-98 ©1990 Harlequin Enterprises Limited

**For a limited time, Harlequin and Silhouette
have an offer you just can't refuse.**

In November and December 1998:

BUY **ANY** TWO HARLEQUIN
OR SILHOUETTE BOOKS and
SAVE $10.00
off future purchases

OR BUY ANY THREE HARLEQUIN OR SILHOUETTE BOOKS
AND **SAVE $20.00** OFF FUTURE PURCHASES!

(each coupon is good for $1.00 off the purchase of two
Harlequin or Silhouette books)

....

JUST BUY 2 HARLEQUIN OR SILHOUETTE BOOKS, SEND US YOUR
NAME, ADDRESS AND 2 PROOFS OF PURCHASE (CASH REGISTER
RECEIPTS) AND HARLEQUIN WILL SEND YOU A COUPON BOOKLET
WORTH **$10.00** OFF FUTURE PURCHASES OF HARLEQUIN OR
SILHOUETTE BOOKS IN 1999. SEND US 3 PROOFS OF PURCHASE AND
WE WILL SEND YOU 2 COUPON BOOKLETS WITH A TOTAL **SAVING OF**
$20.00. (ALLOW 4-6 WEEKS DELIVERY) OFFER EXPIRES
DECEMBER 31, 1998.

....

I accept your offer! Please send me a coupon booklet(s), to:

NAME: _____

ADDRESS: _____

CITY: _____ STATE/PROV.: _____ POSTAL/ZIP CODE: _____

Send your name and address, along with your cash register
receipts for proofs of purchase, to:

In the U.S.	In Canada
Harlequin Books	Harlequin Books
P.O. Box 9057	P.O. Box 622
Buffalo, NY	Fort Erie, Ontario
14269	L2A 5X3

PHQ4982

All new...and filled with the mystery and romance you love!

SOMEBODY'S BABY
by Amanda Stevens in November 1998

A FATHER FOR HER BABY
by B. J. Daniels in December 1998

A FATHER'S LOVE
by Carla Cassidy in January 1999

It all begins one night when three women go into labor in the same Galveston, Texas, hospital. Shortly after the babies are born, fire erupts, and though each child and mother make it to safety, there's more than just the mystery of birth to solve now....

Don't miss this *all new* LOST & FOUND trilogy!

Available at your favorite retail outlet.

HARLEQUIN®
Makes any time special ™